Stage Fright

Erica Field

WEST WIND
Troll Associates

Copyright © 1995 by Robert Hirschfeld.
Cover illustration copyright © 1995 by
Matthew Archambault.

Published by Troll Associates, Inc. WestWind is an imprint of Troll Associates.

Printed in the United States of America.

10   9   8   7   6   5   4   3   2

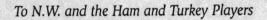

To N.W. and the Ham and Turkey Players

CHAPTER
1

Alison Crisp hated palm trees.

She stood in the dry brown front yard of her new house and glared at the palms along her street. They looked dumb—spindly, hundred-foot trunks with tiny clumps of fronds on top. Definitely not one of Mother Nature's better efforts. Oaks and maples and elms were *real* trees, with graceful branches, beautiful leaves, and lots of shade. These things were a joke. And as for shade, forget it. She sighed and looked down the empty block. Some shade would have been nice. It was only ten in the morning, but it was already way too hot.

At sixteen Alison was tall and slender with brown hair, worn long and straight, framing an oval face. Her hazel eyes could glow with happiness but now they were dull. She kicked a lump of dirt and it crumbled to dust. Like her whole life had crumbled.

The Crisps and their things had arrived in

Southern California from Connecticut a few days before. Most of their boxes were unpacked and the furniture in place. That, at least, looked familiar in the strange rooms.

But nothing else did.

"Believe it or not, this move is a good thing," Mom had said months before. "I'll have to quit my job, but this transfer is too good for your dad to turn down." Mrs. Crisp had written for a local newspaper. "I know you'll miss your friends, and it'll be hard getting used to a new place. But we'll love California. Think about beaches all year round, Ally. No more freezing winters!"

"Right. Look on the bright side," Dad had urged. Eric Crisp was an engineer. "The company may shut the Connecticut plant down, and everyone would be out of work, including me. Good jobs are scarce these days."

None of this logic had impressed Alison's twelve-year-old sister, Dana. She'd started crying the day their parents broke the news, and she'd been crying ever since, resistant to all attempts to cheer her up. Seeing Dana forever moping made Alison resolve not to do likewise. At sixteen she was too old for that kind of thing.

But still . . . she *liked* winter, even if Mom didn't. She'd miss snow falling silently at night and sparkling on roofs and branches. And she loved their big old house with its stone fireplace and attic full of memories, and the oak tree by her bedroom window. Here, there was no fireplace, no upstairs or attic, not even a basement. Her bedroom windows looked out on a bare yard and a high fence separating them from a back yard on the next street.

Mostly Alison missed her friends, especially her best friend, Melanie. Every time she thought of Melanie, three thousand miles away, she had to blink back tears. A big part of her life was gone, leaving an aching emptiness. Alison and Melanie had sworn to stay in touch and see each other on vacations. And they would, at first. Maybe she'd see Melanie at Christmas. But they'd drift apart, and nothing would be the same. Alison's future looked as drab and monotonous as the ugly landscape around her.

"The thing to remember," her dad had said, "is that at least we're in it together. A family."

Yeah, right, she thought. Guess again. Dad was wrapped up in his new job, leaving for work early and getting home late. Mom worried about finding a new job, missed her own friends, and wasn't her usual cheerful self. Dana was in her private cloud of gloom and doom, which depressed Alison even more.

Tears welled up as she plodded back to the house. But she suddenly realized her eyes were burning and the tears had nothing to do with her mood. What . . . ?

"Smog's getting you, huh? It's bad today."

Startled, Alison turned—and stared. A girl stood on the sidewalk, her black hair pinned up in a sleek coil. She had large brown eyes under dark brows, and deeply tanned skin. She looked about

Alison's age. It was her clothes which made Alison gawk: a full, ankle-length maroon velour skirt, the edge of a petticoat just visible underneath. Under a matching laced bodice, she wore a frilly white blouse with puffy sleeves. Last and weirdest was a pair of chunky army boots. She looked like she was going to a costume party, but that wasn't likely at ten A.M.

Alison knew she was staring and was embarrassed. But if the other girl knew she was being stared at, she didn't look embarrassed at all.

"Are you our new neighbor? I'm Kayla Martínez."

"Yeah, I guess so. My name's Alison Crisp. Is smog what's making my eyes water? Please don't say it's always like this."

"It's usually not this bad," said the other girl, shaking her head and wrinkling her nose with distaste. "Look at the ridge there. When the air's only a little yellow, it's okay. But when it's brown like that, yuck!" She pointed down the street, which rose gently into low foothills.

Alison turned and saw the ridge outlined by a muddy haze. "Gross!" She studied the other girl. "It doesn't seem to bother you any."

"I'm lucky," Kayla said. "But my aunt can't go outside at all on days like this. We live on the corner there." She jerked a thumb toward a pink stucco house with a red tile roof. "Where are you from?"

"Connecticut." Just saying the name of the state made Alison feel homesick.

Kayla twirled around and the skirt billowed. "What thinkest thou of my dress? Is it not passing fair? Methinks it highly fetching."

Alison blinked.

"Insooth, is it not pleasing to thine eye?"

Alison wondered if the smog was affecting her brain or her ears. What was Kayla saying? Was this some kind of California slang?

The other girl saw Alison's confusion and put a hand to her mouth. "Oops! Sorry. I'm practicing my old-time speech, getting ready for Merrie Olde England. I was asking whether you liked my dress."

"It's very . . . nice. Did you say you're going to England?" Alison asked, still confused.

"I wish," Kayla sighed. "No, just 'Merrie Olde England.' *Merrie* with an *i-e*, and *Olde* with an *e* at the end. It's sort of a historical theme park that's held on weekends every summer at a ranch ten miles from here. It's set up like an English village in Shakespeare's time. There's entertainment and food and crafts and everyone dresses in old-time clothes, like mine. I made this myself. I'm going to work there this year—I hope."

Light dawned for Alison. "Oh, I get it. And everybody who goes to Olde England—"

"*Merrie* Olde England," Kayla corrected. "M. O. E. or MOE for short."

"And everyone has to dress up like that, huh?"

"The ones who work there do. Customers don't have to, but lots of them do, anyway. They like pretending they're in England in 1600. It's kind of neat."

Alison didn't think wearing heavy old clothes in hot weather and talking funny was such a great way to pass the time, but she kept her thoughts to herself.

"Are the boots historical, too?" she asked.

"No, just practical." Kayla grinned. "I'm going there with my parents to help set up their booth. It'll be all muddy and dusty, so I'm saving my good shoes."

"Do your parents work there?"

"Yeah. They sell handmade leather goods like belts and purses. Kaye does the designs, and she and Larry both do the work. The rest of the year they sell stuff to boutiques."

"Kaye and Larry—they're your parents?"

Kayla nodded. "That's how I got my name—*Kay* from Kaye, and *la* from Larry. It's also their brand name: Kayla Krafts. Anything else you want to know?"

"How can it be muddy and dusty at the same time?"

"They water the dirt streets to keep the dust down. That makes it muddy, but there's a lot of dust anyway. Probably from the hay bales."

Every time Kayla explained one thing, Alison found herself mystified by something else. "Hay bales?"

"Thousands of them. That's what you sit on."

"Why? Didn't they have chairs back then?"

"Sure, but it's outdoors. Folding chairs are too modern. Hay bales can stay outside and not get ruined. It's like old-time lawn furniture."

"Sounds . . . different."

Kayla's eyes lit up. "Listen, we're leaving soon. Come with us and check it out!"

Alison's first impulse was to say no. She wasn't about to put on a forty-pound dress and run around in dusty mud, or muddy dust. But then she thought: what else was there to do today? Or tomorrow or the next day? Kayla seemed okay; at worst she'd be bored for a few hours and back where she started tomorrow, looking at a future full of smog and loneliness.

"I'll check with my mom," Alison said. "But I don't have a costume. And I can't speak old-time English either, with all that *thou* and *methinks*. Is that a problem?"

"Not today," Kayla assured her. "I dressed up to try for a job. Kaye and Larry won't be in costume, and neither will anyone else. You're fine just like that."

"Wait a second, then." Alison ran inside, surprised to find herself looking forward to the trip.

"Mo-o-om!" she yelled.

"In the living room, Ally!" called Mrs. Crisp.

Alison's mother sat reading a gardening catalog. As usual these days, she looked worn-out and edgy.

"Is it okay if I go to a fair with this girl from down the block and her parents?"

"What kind of fair?"

Alison explained Merrie Olde England and Kayla, and what Kayla's family did there.

"I suppose so," said Mrs. Crisp. "Go ahead."

Alison turned, but her mother's voice stopped her.

"Ally, wait!" her mother exclaimed. "Why not take Dana along?" Loud rock music boomed from down the hall, and Mrs. Crisp winced. "She's in her room."

Alison started to protest, but thought better of it. Maybe Dana would brighten up if she had something interesting to do.

Her sister was lying on the floor of her room, staring at the ceiling while one of Alison's favorite CDs blared from her stereo. Alison fought off the urge to yell at her for taking the CD without asking first.

"Want to come to a fair?" she yelled over the music.

Dana was silent. It wasn't clear if she'd even heard. Alison turned down the stereo on Dana's desk, getting an angry look in response.

"I'm listening! What do you want, anyway?"

Alison kept her cool. There was no sense in both of them acting like brats. "You want to come with me and a girl I just met to this fair? Everyone dresses up like in *Robin Hood*, and talks old-time English."

Dana sneered. "It sounds stupid."

"It's something to do. How about it?"

"No." Dana pouted. "Turn the music back up and leave me alone. Close the door on your way out."

"With pleasure," muttered Alison. She turned the volume up and left her sister to her misery.

"She'd rather sulk," she told Mrs. Crisp.

Mrs. Crisp frowned. "Well, don't be too late."

Alison went out, relieved to get away and wondering if her family would ever get back to normal.

"Come on! We're almost ready," Kayla called from the end of the block.

A battered old van sat in the Martínez driveway, its rear doors open. As Alison approached someone came out of the house with a stack of cartons so big that all she could see was the person's legs, in faded jeans and dusty boots. The walking pile maneuvered itself to the back of the van. Freed from his burden, a man came down the driveway, wiping sweat off his face with a blue bandanna and greeting Alison with a smile.

"Hi! I'm Larry Martínez, and you must be Alison. Glad you're joining us!"

Larry Martínez was tall, with dark eyes like his daughter's. He wore a loose-fitting print shirt and jeans cinched with a broad leather belt embossed with a complicated design. Wisps of blond hair stuck out from under a broad-brimmed leather hat with a braided leather band.

"Let's get this show on the road, okay?" Larry called back to the house.

"Coming!" called a woman from inside. A moment later she emerged with a wooden box of tools. She shoved it into the back of the van and slammed the rear doors. She was shorter than Alison, with short curly reddish hair.

"I'm Kaye. Nice to meet you." She peered at

Alison's eyes. "Smog's getting to you, huh? It won't be so bad at the fairgrounds. Ready to go?"

"Sure," Alison replied.

Mr. Martínez opened the driver's-side back door. "There's room for the two of you next to the belts."

Kayla peered in past her father and frowned. "If I get squeezed, I'm going to ruin my skirt."

"I told you not to put it on yet," said her mother, shaking her head. "Take it off and put it in back."

"Okay," muttered Kayla, yanking off her boots. "I was just getting into the mood." She pulled off her skirt and Alison saw that she had on shorts underneath.

The costume stowed away, they got in and headed for the highway—oops, thought Alison, they call them freeways here.

"I like your hat," Alison said to Mr. Martínez. "And the belt. Did you make them?"

"I made the hat. Kaye made the belt."

"That hat isn't Old English, is it?" asked Alison.

"Afraid not," said Mrs. Martínez, turning to face her. "At the fair we show mostly belts and bags. The hats are stashed away unless a customer asks for them. That way we don't get in trouble with the history police."

"History police?"

"The people who run the fair have a thing about authenticity. They check up on everyone. If you're caught wearing a watch, that's bad."

"Another thing," Kayla told Alison. "Don't call

the fair 'MOE' around strangers. They might think you're making fun, and some of them take it really seriously. Like Elissa Yarborough, the boss, and her assistant, Derek Kimball. They call him the master of the revels, and he's very . . . well, you'll see."

They exited from the freeway near a handmade sign reading MERRIE OLDE ENGLAND, onto a narrower road that wound along under a heavy growth of evergreens. More signs indicated that they were nearing the fair. After a few miles, Mr. Martínez swung into a driveway under a wooden arch reading YE OLDE PARKING LOT.

The driveway opened into a gigantic clearing of graded earth with a few cars, trucks, and vans huddled at the far end. "On Saturday, when they open for business, this lot will be jammed," Kayla said.

They parked by the other vehicles, and several of the people who were unloading them smiled and waved.

A round man with a bushy black beard and an apron over khaki pants and a Merrie Olde England T-shirt looked up from the back of the truck next to them.

"Yo, how you doing? I'll be around later to buy one of your fancy belts."

Mr. Martínez laughed as he opened the van's rear doors. "It'll have to be made to order, Oscar. We don't have your size. You selling beef ribs and chicken again?"

"You bet," boomed Oscar, hefting a large carton. "Best Old English barbecue you'll ever taste!"

As he walked away, Kayla whispered, "He makes great chicken, but skip the beef ribs."

"Give you good day, gentlefolk!" The strangest man Alison had ever seen was walking toward them. He wore a velvety green jacket with flecks of gold thread, short baggy red pants that ended above his knees, and white tights. Around his neck was a huge white frilly ruff which looked terribly uncomfortable. The pointed toes of his shoes curled up in front. Alison stifled a giggle as he turned to Mrs. Martínez, swept off a big plumed hat, and bowed deeply.

"Lady, thou art as fair a sight as mine eyes have beheld this morn! 'Tis a passing fine day, is't not?"

Mrs. Martínez gave the man a slight smile. "Hello, Derek. Nice to see you, too. Yes, the weather's great."

She turned. "Alison, meet Derek Kimball, the master of the revels. Derek, this is Alison Crisp."

"Hi," Alison said.

The man made another bow, brushing the dirt with his plume. His brown hair was combed over his forehead, and his little mustache and beard reminded Alison of a picture she'd seen of Shakespeare.

"Milady, how fare ye this morrow? Alison Crisp—'tis a sweet-sounding name!"

"Um . . ." Alison wasn't sure how to respond. "I . . . I like your clothes. Neat hat."

Derek flushed with pleasure. "Thanks! Uh, that is, gramercy for thy kind words. 'Tis my own design."

"Hi, Derek," Mr. Martínez said. "Got to get to work."

Derek nodded and then frowned. "Larry, that hat . . . it's not exactly authentic."

Mr. Martínez raised a hand. "It's just for today."

"Well, good. We mustn't spoil the illusion, hmm?"

"Of course not," said Mrs. Martínez. "See you later."

"Good day, gentlefolk." Derek bustled off.

"Wow!" Alison said, staring after him.

"I was going to describe him," Kayla said, "but I decided it'd be better to see for yourself."

"I thought no one'd be dressed like that . . . or talking like that."

Kayla grinned. "Derek doesn't count. I bet he talks like that at home and sleeps in costume."

"Truly bizarre."

Mrs. Martínez put an arm around her daughter's shoulders. "Some people like a make-believe world better than the real one. It's a little strange, but harmless."

"Alison," said Mr. Martínez, "why don't you take a look around while Kayla helps us set up? You'll probably see some performers working on their acts."

"I could help out, too," Alison offered.

"Not necessary," replied Mrs. Martínez. "You're our guest, and it's a hot day."

"Go on," Kayla urged. "I'll find you later and introduce you to everyone. If anyone asks, you're with us. Go to the main stage, where the performers are."

Alison followed Kayla's directions down a dirt path lined with booths where people were painting signs, arranging crafts, and setting up equipment. Hearing music, she turned that way. The path *was* muddy and there was dust in the air, just as Kayla had said. Hay bales were everywhere, big enough for two to sit on if they didn't mind crowding.

The music grew louder. It sounded like a brass band. Alison followed the music to a large grove of trees and veered off the path into the woods.

Abruptly, it became shady and cool. The trees were old oaks, she thought, beautiful and enormous, with huge knotty branches that met overhead. It was just like walking through a leafy tunnel.

Alison stood still, just enjoying the moment. Her eyes had stopped bothering her, it was quiet and peaceful here, and the music was soothing.

This place wasn't so bad, she thought. Most of the people seemed friendly enough, even if some of them were a little strange, like Derek. It might be nice to come again when the fair was actually happening. Maybe she'd—

"Who goes there?" someone yelled.

Startled, Alison whirled around, but there was nobody there. Yet the voice had been very close. In fact, it had seemed to come from somewhere above her.

"Aha!" the voice yelled. Alison screamed as a grotesque face suddenly appeared directly in front of her, hanging upside-down in the air.

2

Alison's heart pounded, and she tried to remain calm. It's only a person, she told herself, nothing to get hysterical about. Only a crazy person with a hideous face hanging upside-down in front of her. Faces look weird upside down, and this one was like a black-and-white mask, which made it even weirder. Finally, she could trust herself to speak.

"Very funny, whoever you are!"

The face disappeared and the leaves rustled. Then a boy dropped lightly to the ground and faced her, arms folded, with a cocky grin. He wore white makeup, and his features were outlined in black.

"Actually, I *am* pretty funny," he said, brushing a stray curl of dark hair out of his eyes. "More fun than a barrel of monkeys. A regular laugh riot. Ask anybody."

It was impossible for Alison to tell his age or

what he looked like under the paint, except that his eyes were green, and his shaggy hair was long. He was long-legged and wiry, a little taller than Alison.

"So scaring people to death is your idea of humor. Great. Why don't you climb back into your tree?" She started to walk away, feeling angry and embarrassed.

He called, "Lighten up! You survived, right?"

Alison gave him a chilly look. "No big deal. And by the way, that makeup looks really dumb."

The boy glared. "Thanks. I'll keep it in mind."

"You're a performer here?"

"You must be new, or you'd know about me."

Alison found his arrogance annoying. "Well, I don't. Sorry about that."

He bowed, more naturally and gracefully than Derek. "Robin Goodfellow at your service: jester, juggler, general nuisance." From his bow he moved into a handstand, then backflipped to his feet. "What's your name? Do you work here?"

"Alison. I'm just visiting." She told him about coming with Kayla and her parents.

"Sure, last year I bought one of Kaye's belts. So, what are you doing now?"

"I was on my way to the main stage."

"I'll take you. You shouldn't be in the forest alone. There are bandits and dragons lying in wait for young damsels. Shall we?" He invited her to precede him with a sweep of an arm. Alison hesitated, irritated at his attitude, then decided that he was harmless and agreed.

They came out of the trees behind the stage. All Alison could see was a tall wooden structure and a gigantic burlap tent pitched next to it. People came and went through a flap in the tent.

Alison and Robin walked around to the front. The main stage was big enough to hold the entire Crisp house and yard, with plenty of room left over. The back wall looked like a castle, with windowed towers at the ends and a little railed balcony over two huge wooden doors in the middle. Colorful banners hung on poles along the top of the wall. In a corner of the stage, six musicians played brass instruments. A man and a woman watched four pairs of dancers doing something that involved a lot of leaping. Every time the dancers came down, the stage thudded.

The audience seats were hay bales, hundreds of them arranged in rows. Men were dumping more bales from a truck and wrestling them into place.

"No!" called the woman, signaling to stop the music. "More energy, people. And *smile*, you're enjoying yourselves. Once again, from the top."

The musicians groaned. One clutched his throat and staggered around the stage. "Water!" he croaked. "Or cold beer!"

The woman looked stone-faced. "Very amusing, Wolfgang. Now, can we get back to work?"

"Wolfgang?" Alison whispered.

"That's his name. Really," Robin whispered back.

Wolfgang snapped to rigid attention and saluted. "Yes, ma'am, right away, ma'am. I regret that I only have one life to give to MOE."

"Don't use that name, please," said the woman.

Wolfgang trudged back to the band, who applauded. He stopped, catching sight of Robin.

"What ho, clown! Who's your friend?"

"What ho, Wolfgang. This is Alison," said Robin. "Meet Wolfgang, of Her Majesty's Wind Ensemble."

Wolfgang waved to her. "What ho, Alison!"

Alison waved back. "What ho to you, too."

"Robin, please! We're working," called the woman. "From the top."

Alison and Robin sat down to watch. The dancers wore rigid smiles and clenched teeth. Their breathing was labored and they grunted when they jumped.

"That's hard work," she commented.

"You bet," answered Robin. "Think how it'll be when they're wearing fancy outfits that weigh a ton. And thin-soled shoes, on a stage that's like a giant griddle in this heat. They may smile on the outside, but they're broiling on the inside."

"Do you perform here?" she asked.

"Nope. I work the streets. Get a small crowd, do some juggling, some jokes, maybe a tumbling run, pass the hat, and move on."

Suddenly a shadow fell over Alison. "Well, well. Look who's here. So you're back, huh?"

Alison looked up to find a man looming over

her. He wore jeans and a Merrie Olde England T-shirt with the sleeves rolled up over muscular, tattooed arms. Strapped to his belt was a walkie-talkie. He had a jutting jaw, very light blue eyes, and hair shaved to stubble. His smile held no warmth.

Robin stood up, and Alison did the same. "Hey, Billy. Going to be keeping us in line again?"

"I'm still head of security." Billy flicked a glance at Alison. "Does she have business here?"

"She's just visiting," Robin replied tightly. "I'm showing her around."

Billy frowned. "When we're getting ready to open, we don't want a lot of outsiders underfoot. You should know better. She can't stay."

"Come on!" protested Robin. "We're not in the way. And Alison's not 'a bunch of outsiders.' She's one girl and she came with the Martínezes."

Billy folded his massive arms across his chest. "They bring an extra person, somebody else brings another, and suddenly we're crawling with people who have no business here. She goes. Now."

Alison felt very uncomfortable. "That's okay," she said, "I'll leave."

"Wait a second," snapped Robin. "You don't have to go anywhere. You're with me."

Sneering, Billy shook his head. "You haven't changed, have you? You're still the same wise guy who thinks he can do anything he wants."

"And you still get off on bossing people around," retorted Robin, not giving an inch.

Alison saw the dancers and musicians watching

the confrontation. She wished she were invisible, or better yet, that she'd stayed home. Robin had put her in the middle of something that was basically none of her business.

Billy turned away from Robin, saying, "I don't have time for this garbage." His cold gaze fastened on Alison. "You'll have to leave."

"Why don't you go find someone else to pick on?" Robin asked.

Billy looked around. All activity by the stage had stopped, and everyone was watching him and Robin. He pulled out his walkie-talkie. "I'm going to have you escorted out of here," he growled.

But then Billy froze at the sight of something behind Robin. Alison saw Derek, in his gaudy getup, coming toward them through the hay bales. With him was a woman, short and plump, in a loose, flower-print dress and sandals. She had apple cheeks and brown hair done up in a bun.

"What's happening, Billy?" the woman asked.

Billy put the walkie-talkie back. "Nothing I can't handle, Ms. Bustard. I was telling this girl to leave, and he gave me grief." He fixed Robin with a nasty stare.

"We weren't in the way," Robin protested. "We were minding our own business and Billy hassled us for no reason at all."

"That's a lie!" Billy shouted. "I was doing my job and she and him, they were out of line!"

"She and *he*," murmured Derek. No one paid him any attention.

The woman looked at Robin coolly. "It's a hot

day and we're all edgy. Robin, you must cooperate with our security staff. Billy, that will be all for now."

Billy started to object, then thought better of it. "Okay, fine. I'm outta here."

He shot Robin a last murderous look and walked off. Ms. Bustard waited until he was out of earshot. Then she asked, "Honestly, Robin. Why must you goad him all the time? Billy is a little touchy—"

"He's a jerk on a power trip," Robin cut in. "He gives people a hard time even when they're not doing anything wrong. He ought to be fired."

The woman smiled thinly. "It's funny, but I've heard others say the same thing about you."

Robin looked hurt. "Me?"

"Yes, you. If your act weren't so popular, you'd be out. You get on people's nerves and you mock everything Merrie Olde England stands for."

Robin stuck out his lower lip, reminding Alison of her kid sister. "Some people have no sense of humor."

"And some people have no sense, period," the woman retorted. "Picking on Billy is foolish. He has a bad temper, and he's twice your size."

"Okay," Robin conceded. "I'll try to be nice."

"That would be wise." She turned to Alison. "Hello. I don't think we've met."

"Alison Crisp, Gwendolyn Bustard," said Robin. "And Derek Kimball."

"I met you before," Alison told Derek. "I was with Kayla Martínez, remember?"

"Yea, verily, as though 'twere but minutes ago," said Derek.

It *was* only minutes ago, Alison thought.

The dark-haired woman came forward, peering at Alison intently enough to make her ill at ease.

"Tell me," she said, "have you a job here?" Her voice was beautiful and rich.

"Well, no. I just came out to look around."

"Oh, here you are!" Kayla, now in her homemade costume, ran up, holding her skirt high to keep it out of the dirt. "Larry and Kaye told me to take off, and I thought you might be here. I was going to introduce you around, but I see you're doing okay on your own."

"And you are . . ." asked Gwendolyn.

"Kayla Martínez. My parents do leather crafts."

"Of course," said Gwendolyn. "How silly of me to forget. Alison, you would make a lovely addition to my court, with that hair and complexion."

"Court?" asked Alison, feeling self-conscious.

Derek explained. "Gwen has been Queen Elizabeth here for fifteen years. This year, two of our ladies-in-waiting have to be replaced. Are you interested?"

Alison didn't know what to think, or say. The invitation had come as a complete surprise.

"Gee, I—I don't know . . ."

"The pay is low," said the woman, "but the duties are light, and the dresses are stunning."

Alison pondered. Working here and earning money had its attractions. Then she saw Robin trying to catch her eye, giving her little shakes of his head.

Didn't he want her to take the job? And anyway, was it any of his business?

"You need *two* ladies-in-waiting?" asked Kayla. "How about me? My folks drive here every day, so they could take us both. I even have my own dress and I can do a fantastic curtsy."

She demonstrated, stretching one leg straight in front of her and dipping until she was almost sitting on the ground.

"See?" she said.

"Very nice, Kayla," said Gwendolyn. "I'll speak to Elissa about hiring you, but you'll have to wear one of our dresses. Alison? What do you say?"

Robin was still shaking his head. What was his problem? Who cares what he thinks, anyway? she asked herself, still angry at him for involving her in his own problem with Billy. She smiled at Gwendolyn. "I'll ask my parents, and if they say yes, I'll do it."

"Fantastic!" said Kayla.

"Splendid!" said Gwendolyn.

"Forsooth!" said Derek.

Robin didn't say anything.

Gwendolyn fished a card from her purse and gave it to Alison. "Call me tonight. I'll ask Elissa to set up fittings and lessons in being ladies-in-waiting."

"Thanks." Alison stuffed the paper in her pocket.

"We'll have lots of fun," Gwendolyn said with a twinkling smile as she and Derek left.

Alison turned to Robin. "What were you trying to tell me? Did you want me to turn the job down?"

"Right," he said.

"Why?" Kayla demanded. "This morning Alison was standing around rubbing smog out of her eyes. Now she's going to be a lady-in-waiting in the queen's court and wear a gorgeous gown and earn money!"

"Right," Robin agreed.

"Then what's the problem?" asked Alison.

"The only problem with being in Queen Elizabeth's court," Robin replied, "is Queen Elizabeth."

The girls looked at him, then at each other.

"What's that supposed to mean?" asked Alison.

"You'll see," Robin said darkly.

"Stop being such a know-it-all!" snapped Alison, annoyed at his superior air. "And thanks a lot for getting me mixed up in your feud with Billy!"

Robin gaped at her. "You're mad at *me?* I stood up for you when Billy the Bully tried to kick you out!"

"You embarrassed me and made a big deal out of nothing." Alison grew angry all over again, thinking about it. "It had nothing to do with me! You were more interested in giving him a hard time than in how I felt. And I'm taking the job as a lady-in-waiting!"

Robin threw up his hands. "Back off, okay? Go ahead, take the job, but you won't like it."

Alison glared. "Thanks for the encouragement."

"Did something happen between you and Billy

Hawley?" Kayla asked Robin. "I saw him as I was coming here, and he looked really mad."

Robin shrugged. "He tried his Big Boss Man routine and I didn't let him get away with it."

Kayla looked concerned. "I'd watch out for him. I hate to think what he might do to someone he has it in for. Billy's even nasty to his friends."

"I can handle Billy," insisted Robin.

"Uh, Robin, one other thing," Kayla added. "About your makeup . . . it . . . I don't think . . ."

"I'm going to take it off," Robin muttered.

"What ho, Robin!" The dance rehearsal was over, and Wolfgang squatted at the edge of the stage.

"Robin, I saw you and Billy almost get into it a few minutes ago. Be careful with that guy," Wolfgang advised.

Robin scowled. "Come on, take it easy, will you? You're all making too big a deal out of this."

But Wolfgang shook his head. "No, really," he persisted. "Remember Tom, our tuba player from last year? Billy hated him for some reason. He got on Tom's case every day, and wound up scaring him so bad he didn't come back this year."

"Uh-huh," said Robin, "and Billy chews nails and kicks puppies and cheats at cards. You made your point, he's a tough guy. Look, I don't want a showdown with Billy, but I won't let him push me around."

"All right," Wolfgang said. "But I'd hate to see anything happen to you. Nobody else here plays chess. By the way, what's that strange stuff on your face?"

"Okay, all right, I give up!" Robin shouted, drawing startled glances from the dancers. "It was a rotten idea, I shouldn't have put it on, and I'm going take it off right now. And I'll never do it again. Are you happy now? Everyone around here is a critic!"

He stomped away toward the rear of the stage.

Wolfgang stood up. "Touchy, isn't he?"

"Is Billy really dangerous?" asked Alison.

Wolfgang considered for a moment. "He's mean and sneaky. Last year when he was bullying our tuba player, he was careful not to do anything while Elissa or any of the honchos were there. As long as Robin's with other people, he's all right. But if Billy finds him alone and thinks he can get away with it, I don't know."

"Wolfgang!" Another musician was calling him from the rear of the stage.

"What ho!"

"Let's go. We have to rehearse the fanfares for the Queen's Pageant."

Wolfgang made a face. "I hate rehearsal days. They're always hot and confused and the refreshment stands haven't opened for business yet. See you."

Kayla and Alison waved to him. "Will your parents let you do the fair?" asked Kayla.

"I'm pretty sure. They're so into their own problems, they'll be happy to have me off their hands. And maybe we can bring my sister Dana one day. She's been totally depressed since we got to California."

"Good idea. Hey, are you hungry? I'm starved."

Alison realized that she hadn't eaten since breakfast, and that had been a long time ago.

"Me, too. Where can we get something to eat?"

"I bet Manny is open for business."

"What does he sell?"

"Meat pies, for the customers. For people who work here, he makes burritos and churros."

"I know what a burrito is," Alison said. "But what's a churro?"

"They're sort of like doughnuts, except they're long and thin. Manny fries them till they're hot and crisp and dusts them with sugar."

Suddenly, Alison was ravenous. "What are we standing around for? Let's get some!"

Later, after sharing a huge chicken burrito, Alison and Kayla nibbled churros. Around them the fair hummed with activity as finishing touches were applied to booths, performers hurried here and there, and workers sprinkled water on the streets to keep the dust down. It was midafternoon and the heat was stifling.

"I should check with Larry and Kaye," said Kayla. "They'll probably be ready to leave in about an hour."

"I think I'll look around some more," Alison replied. "I'll meet you by the van in an hour."

Alison went past the main stage, where a group of actors was rehearsing a comedy that involved a lot of falling down, arm-waving, and shouting. She passed the big tent, which she figured was probably the performers' dressing area, and found herself in the grove where she had met Robin.

It was cool and quiet under the old trees. Alison sat with her back against the trunk of an oak tree and thought about her day. On the whole it had been pretty good. She had a friend, a place to go, even a job! Almost everyone she had met seemed nice. Well, Derek was strange. And she didn't like Billy, though maybe he wasn't so bad when Robin wasn't teasing him. Robin might be talented, but he was also infuriating, thoughtless, and smug.

Alison yawned. What did Robin look like without that silly makeup, she wondered. While thinking about this, she drifted off to sleep, and a dream.

She was walking alone on a path through a gloomy forest. The trees towered over her, making her feel very small. No sunshine penetrated the thick foliage far above her head. A hum of conversation came from somewhere, but Alison couldn't make out the words. Where were the people, and what were they talking about?

Suddenly, a hulking shadow dodged between two trees, too quickly for her to see who—or what—it was. Alison felt a stab of panic. Two of the murmuring voices became louder and she listened.

"We have to put fear into her," someone said. "Even if people are hurt . . . or worse."

"I'm not a violent person," said someone else.

"Relax," said the first voice. "I'll take care of it. If someone dies, that's the way it is."

Alison's eyes popped open. Oak branches

arched over her, and underneath was damp earth and leaves. But the grove which had seemed cool and inviting now felt gloomy and oppressive. Alison wondered how long she had slept. She hadn't brought her watch. Were Kayla and her parents looking for her? She scrambled to her feet, brushing herself off.

If someone dies, that's the way it is. The dream voice had sounded very real and familiar. Had she actually heard it?

Alison burst out of the grove into heat and light and activity. Her feeling of dread began to lighten.

"Hey! What were you doing in those trees?"

Billy, the muscular head of security, loomed over her, looking nasty. "I asked you a question. What you were doing in there?"

"N-nothing," she stammered. "Getting some shade."

"You have no business here. Beat it!"

"Actually, it turns out I *do* have business here," Alison said, trying to meet Billy's cold stare. "I'm going to be one of the queen's ladies-in-waiting."

The notion clearly didn't please Billy. He studied her for a moment, and said, "Well, don't get out of line. I'll be watching you."

As Billy walked away, Alison began to think about her dream, and the menacing voices. They'd seemed so real. But dreams often did. And this one was too bizarre to have been anything but a bad dream. No way could it have been real.

Could it?

CHAPTER

3

As the Martínez van headed home, Kayla turned to Alison. "Wait till you see our dresses. They're from a Hollywood studio wardrobe department. Unbelievable!"

Thinking of Robin's warning about the queen, Alison asked, "How's Ms. Bustard to work with?"

Mr. and Mrs. Martínez exchanged a look.

"Just remember that Gwen takes her role very seriously, and you shouldn't have any problems," Mrs. Martínez said.

"This guy Robin warned me about her," said Alison.

Mrs. Martínez smiled. "Don't take what Robin Goodfellow says at face value, especially about Gwen. They don't get along. He's always needling her, and she—"

Mr. Martínez cut in. "She'd like him fired, because he won't bow to her when she passes by."

"Bow?" Alison wasn't sure she'd heard right.

"Really bow? But . . . it's all pretend, right?"

Mrs. Martínez shrugged. "Gwen says that if she doesn't get the same kind of respect that old English villagers gave the queen, the fair loses its authentic feel."

Mr. Martínez snorted. "Yeah, right! Gwen likes to order people around, which she can't do in real life. She lives for the chance to act like royalty and she hates anyone who won't play along."

Mrs. Martínez gave her husband a sideways glance and sighed. "Larry doesn't like Gwen much. But he's right about one thing: *If* you want to get along with her, you'd better play her game. And if you're going to be in her court, you definitely want to get along with her."

Over a late dinner that night, Alison told her family about her day and her new job. Her parents seemed tired and distracted. Dana picked at her food and moped.

"Eat something, Dana," urged Mr. Crisp. "You really have to eat more."

Dana stared at her plate. "Not hungry."

"Anyway," Alison said, "Merrie Olde England opens Saturday, so you can come see me in the queen's court."

Dana raised her eyebrows in an "are you kidding" expression. "It sounds really dumb."

"Can't do it, honey," said her father. "I'll be at the office on Saturday."

"What?" Mrs. Crisp glared. "Eric, we were going to put up shelves and get those boxes emptied. I'm sick of them lying around."

"You think I *want* to work?" asked Mr. Crisp. "Don't make it harder for me than it already is."

"I'm sorry I make things hard for you," Mrs. Crisp snapped. "My life is such fun lately, how dare I add to your troubles?" Her mouth tightened into a thin line, and tears shone in her eyes.

The meal was finished in tense silence.

For two days Alison and Kayla had fittings and lessons in court behavior. Alison's dress was burgundy, with a full silky skirt and stiff petticoats underneath. The silk brocade bodice was ornately trimmed in gold. Kayla's gown was a similar style in apple green.

With the other four ladies-in-waiting, they did posture work on the main stage under Derek's guidance.

"Shoulders back, heads high." He tugged at Alison and tilted her chin up with a finger. "Young English noblewomen do not carry themselves like milkmaids or serving wenches. Maxine, ladies *never* chew gum!"

"Sorry." Maxine Tsu tossed her gum in the trash.

"Now, curtsy, please."

Alison watched the others fold gracefully down until their upper bodies rested on a circle of silk and crinoline. She tried, but stumbled backward and hit the plywood stage with an embarrassing thud.

"Oh, dear." Derek helped Alison up. "Sabrina, help Alison with her curtsy. You others can rest."

Eighteen-year-old Sabrina Engel was the senior lady-in-waiting. "It's not that hard," she said. "Hold your left knee straight and slide that leg forward as you bend your right knee. Keep your weight centered and don't lean back. Then bend at the waist." She demonstrated in slow motion.

Alison learned quickly. As she did a proper curtsy, the sound of clapping startled her so much, she nearly fell. A slender young man with dark, shaggy hair stood near her, applauding and grinning. It was Robin, without the black and white paint. Alison felt self-conscious and irritated.

"That was maah-velous," he said, still clapping.

Alison didn't smile. "You looked better with the makeup," she snapped. Actually, he *was* cute, with angular features softened by dimples. But she knew she'd die before letting him know it.

"How now, Lady Sabrina," Robin drawled in a mock-British accent. "Is her Majestic Highness around, or is she getting another coat of lacquer?"

Sabrina's smile was chilly. "Bug off, Robin."

He gasped and staggered back. "Oooh, that hurt! Alison, remember: Yes, Your Majesty, no, Your Majesty, whatever Your Majesty says, Your Majesty. Then roll over, and she'll pat your head and give you a treat."

"Ignore him," said Sabrina. "Everyone else does."

"What ho, Robin!" Wolfgang stuck his head through a curtain at the back of the stage. "Chess?"

"You're on." Robin grinned at Alison. "Bye!" He ran backstage through the curtains.

"He gets on my nerves," Alison muttered. "Him and his gigantic ego."

Sabrina smiled. "I guess. But the crowds love him, or he'd be out of here. Gwen doesn't . . ."

She stopped, smiled over Alison's shoulder, and curtsied. Turning, Alison saw Ms. Bustard walking onto the stage, dressed in another flower-print dress and sandals.

"Oh, hi!" Alison said.

"Curtsy to Her Majesty," prompted Sabrina in a low voice, without rising from the floor.

Slightly mystified, Alison did as she was told.

"Lovely, Alison. From this point on, why not address me as Your Majesty—just to get in practice?"

"Uh, sure, Ms. . . . Your Majesty."

Gwendolyn smiled. "When you have time, dear, come backstage and meet Elissa."

She ducked through the curtains and was gone.

"Is that for real?" Alison kept her voice low. "The 'Your Majesty' stuff?"

Sabrina spoke in a whisper. "Believe it. As far as we're concerned, she's Queen Elizabeth. Period. Don't forget, and don't joke about it. *Ever.*"

"Or what?"

"Or she'll make your life miserable. Better go, she wants you."

"She said when I have time."

Sabrina sighed. "She said when you have time,

but she meant now. Go on, we're finished anyway."

Alison weighed this new view of Gwendolyn as she stepped through the curtains. Sure enough, there she stood, with two other people, arms folded, clearly waiting. Kayla saw Alison and ran to join her.

"These are my new court ladies," Gwendolyn purred. "Alison, Kayla, meet Elissa Yarborough."

Elissa, tall and tan in faded denim, smiled. Her long brown hair hung in a braid.

"Hi, Alison. Kayla, don't your parents do those wonderful leather goods?"

"Right, Ms. Yarborough."

Elissa turned to a man at her side. "This is our lord mayor, Zachary Connors. You'll see a lot of him."

Alison thought he was very handsome. His face seemed chiseled out of mahogany, topped by close-cropped curly hair, gray at the temples. He was tall, with broad shoulders and a massive upper body.

"Kayla, Alison, how do you do?" His voice was deep and resonant.

"Do we call you My Lord or Your Honor?" Alison asked.

He chuckled. "Zach will do, backstage."

Quite a difference from Gwen, thought Alison.

"Elissa! A word, please!"

Derek trotted up, trailed by a man in a suit.

Elissa didn't seem delighted to see him. "What is it, Derek? I'm pretty busy right now."

"Elissa, I just heard country-western music! And there's a booth selling soft ice cream! In Elizabethan England! I ask you!"

"Soft ice cream will sell," Elissa pointed out. "And 'Greensleeves' as a country-western song is cute. We're here to entertain, right?"

Derek's hands fluttered. "But—"

Elissa waved him off. "Derek, don't start this argument again. This isn't a museum, it's a fair."

The man in the suit came forward. "Ms. Yarborough, hello." He offered a hand which she ignored. "I have good news."

"I doubt it, Eric." Elissa looked around. "Zach, Gwen, you know Eric Sinclair, the developer?"

Derek sneered at Sinclair, who ignored him. "I'm upping my bid to six hundred thou. What do you say?"

"The same thing I always say, Mr. Sinclair. Our lease here has twelve years to run, and Merrie Olde England will be here for every one of those years."

"Well said," murmured Derek.

Eric Sinclair's lips tightened. "I hoped to keep this friendly, Elissa. Too bad. For both of us."

Elissa met Sinclair's look. "Is that a threat?"

Alison looked at Kayla. What was going on here?

"I don't make threats," said the developer. "But some folks aren't as nice as me. See you, Elissa."

He walked off.

"Bravo!" Derek beamed. "The man is a

walking cash register, a Philistine. Now, about that ice cream . . ."

"No, Derek." Elissa checked her watch. "I have to run. See you all later." She strode away.

Gwendolyn spoke. "Alison, tell the girls I want you all here in twenty minutes, exactly."

"Yes . . . Your Majesty."

Gwendolyn took Derek's arm and moved off, talking to him quietly. Kayla gave Alison a puzzled look.

"Your Majesty?"

"We call her that from here on. Her orders."

Kayla gaped at her. "But she's not queen yet! And what's with Mr. Sinclair? He sounded—"

She broke off, hearing raised voices from the end of the tent. Curious, she and Alison hurried over for a closer look.

Billy Hawley stood rigid, fists clenched, a muscle twitching in his face. Facing him were an angry Robin and a scared Wolfgang. A chessboard lay on the ground, with pieces scattered everywhere.

"Billy, chill out," Wolfgang urged.

"Go blow your horn, wimp," growled Billy. He pointed to Robin. "Come on, wise guy. Right now."

"Billy'll slaughter him," whispered Kayla.

Billy jabbed a finger in Robin's chest. "What's wrong, all mouth and no guts? Take your best shot!"

Without thinking, Alison called out, "Hi, Ms. Yarborough!" staring at a point behind Billy.

The security guard dropped his hands and

spun around, looking for his boss and not finding her.

"She's not here." His pale eyes drilled into Alison, who tried not to flinch.

Alison sensed the danger to Robin was past. If Billy attacked now, it would look unprovoked. "I thought I saw her. Guess I was wrong."

"I remember you," said Billy with an ugly grin. "You're the one who wouldn't leave when I told you to. I'll settle with you another time." He turned to Robin. "You, too, sport. This isn't over." He shoved through the onlookers and was gone.

"Wow," said Kayla, hugging herself and shivering.

Alison sagged in relief. "What was that about?"

"The usual," said Wolfgang, picking up chessmen. "Robin ragged Billy, who went bananas. He kicked over the chess game and would've stomped us if you hadn't stopped him." The musician's face was grim. "Don't put me in the middle of your fights, Robin. Trumpet players can't afford split lips."

"I can handle him!" Robin kicked a hay bale and wheeled on Alison. "And you shouldn't have butted in!"

Alison was stunned. She'd saved him from Billy and made an enemy of the head of security in the process, and this was the thanks she got. "You're welcome," she said icily, walking away.

Robin called, "Hey, wait!" but she kept going.

"He's such a jerk!" she muttered, furious.

"What?" asked Kayla, catching up to her.

"Nothing. Come on, Her Majesty calls."

Kayla touched Alison's arm. "Are you all right?"

Alison shrugged. "Well, let's see: I work with a lady who thinks she's the queen of England, the head of security is a psycho with a grudge against me . . ."

Kayla nodded. "But otherwise everything's okay, huh?"

Alison laughed. "I guess it's just a bad day. Things will get better, right? I mean, they have to."

At eight forty-five A.M. on Opening Day, the Martínezes drove into the employee parking lot. People already waited at the entrance, though the fair didn't open until ten. Red and gold Merrie Olde England banners hung everywhere.

Alison was grumpy. Her parents had said they'd come to the fair "one day." Dana wouldn't even go that far. Alison had been happy to get out of the house without a fight.

"We'll be looking for you in the pageant!" said Mr. Martínez, hugging his daughter. The Queen's Pageant was MOE's biggest, most colorful event, and it took place daily at three P.M.

Mrs. Martínez kissed both girls. "Larry has his camera and he's going to get pictures, history police or not. Good luck!"

The girls walked toward the main stage, past freshly decorated booths. Delicious cooking smells filled the air, and the weather was clear, warm, and sunny.

"Alison! Kayla!" Maxine Tsu and Bonnie Burke ran up. Bonnie, a second-year lady-in-waiting, was eating a churro, and she offered it around. "Today's the day! Let's get into costume!"

"Relax," advised Maxine. "We have hours yet. Hey, there's Robin! Hi, Robin!"

He stood by the path, juggling balls, wearing a black and white checked tunic over black tights, and a green cap with a white plume. Looking up, he caught Alison's eye. She quickly turned away.

"Alison!" he called. "Hey!"

She walked on, aware that the other girls were watching. Suddenly, Robin stood in front of her. He swept off his cap and bowed gracefully.

"Good day, fair lady. Or is it, 'Fair day, good lady'? You're not talking to me anyway, right?"

It seemed to Alison that whenever she and Robin met, she wound up looking and feeling foolish. She felt people's eyes on them and didn't want to talk. "Hello," she said, keeping her voice and expression cool. "Excuse me, I have to go."

She started around him, but he sidestepped and stood in front of her again.

"Please leave me alone," she said.

"Look . . . the other day I was a jerk. I shouldn't have hassled Billy, or you, either. I'm sorry. Okay?"

She nodded. "Okay."

"Then you don't think I'm a total loser?"

Alison shook her head. "Not total."

Robin let out a sigh of relief. "I really am okay. I kiss babies and help old people across streets, even if they don't want to go, and I brush my teeth once a month whether they need it or not. My dog loves me. At least, he says he does. I'm not sure I trust him."

Alison couldn't help laughing, and he smiled.

"I really do have to go," she said.

"See you." Robin walked away, juggling.

Alison's bad mood vanished—until she saw Billy coming toward her with two other security men. Their red and black sleeveless tunics were cinched by broad leather belts with walkie-talkies clipped onto them. The other guards wore shirts under their tunics, but Billy apparently liked to show off his muscles and tattoos.

He stopped talking when he saw her. Alison forced herself to walk on, despite the pale eyes fixed on her. The men passed, and it took all Alison's willpower not to look back after them.

"Let's check out the stage," Kayla said as they neared the performers' tent. They found it festively decorated, with flags hanging over the brightly painted facade.

"Good morrow, fair damsels!" Derek came to the front of the stage and bowed. He was in full master of the revels regalia, his ruff snowy white and a long feather in his cap. "What think you of our village?"

"It looks great!" Kayla climbed onto the stage, and the others followed. Alison gazed at the sea of hay bales. There'll be thousands of people out there, she thought. And I'll be up here. It was nine o'clock—only an hour until opening. She felt a growing excitement.

A few other performers were onstage. She saw Wolfgang and his trumpet, and called out, "What ho!"

He blew a fanfare at her. It was so good to feel a part of it all, she thought, no longer adrift in a world of indifferent strangers. She even felt kindly toward Derek, who was smiling as if he were personally responsible for designing and building the whole place.

"What's that for?" asked Alison, pointing up to a little balcony over the tall double doors in the middle of the facade. It was about ten feet long, and masked by a maroon curtain. "Does anything happen up there?"

"Oh, yes." Derek was glad to have the chance to explain. "It's called the inner above. Theaters in Shakespeare's day used it for intimate scenes. You open the curtain by pulling a rope behind the center doors. Let me show you."

He opened a door and pulled the rope. Alison heard the whir of moving curtains but the balcony overhang blocked her view.

She stepped back for a better look. Then someone behind her screamed.

It was Kayla, staring upward, mouth agape. "What is that thing?" she asked, her voice trembling.

Bonnie joined her, frowning. "Someone's idea of a joke, I guess."

Alison looked up—and gasped. A grotesque stuffed dummy hung from the ceiling of the little balcony, its head tilted at an unnatural angle, its neck in a heavy rope noose. Next to the figure hung a ragged piece of white cloth. A skull and crossbones were daubed on it in red. Under the skull were the words, WATCH OUT.

The dummy had a red wig with a jewelled crown on top. It wore a lavish burgundy silk dress . . . Alison's knees grew rubbery and her heart began to pound.

"That's the queen's crown," whispered Maxine, standing next to Alison.

Kayla nodded. "Uh-huh. Gwendolyn will have a fit. And that dress . . . Alison? Isn't that yours?"

Alison couldn't take her eyes off the effigy. Slowly, she nodded her head, her voice barely a whisper.

"Yes. It's mine."

4

Why my dress? Alison couldn't stop thinking. It wasn't really *her* dress, of course, but she still felt as if she'd been attacked personally. And even though the dress was unharmed, it seemed somehow soiled.

Merrie Olde England was open for business. Alison had watched the opening ceremony, along with a crowd of thousands. Derek had told old English jokes, which no one understood, and Zach, in green and gold with a heavy silver neck chain, had read a proclamation of welcome.

Now, customers walked past vendors hawking crafts and food while strolling musicians serenaded them. Business seemed to be good.

It was almost time for the Mayor's Procession. Everyone checked makeup, hair, and costumes in a row of mirrors. Alison turned to Bonnie at the next mirror. "Where's Her Majesty? I haven't seen her all day."

"Gwen gets ready in Elissa's office."

"Attention, everyone!" called Derek. "People?"

He could hardly be heard over the backstage din.

"Listen up!" boomed Zach. Silence descended.

Derek bobbed his head. "Let's get going, everyone. Get in line, and please, no fooling around."

The procession formed on a hill at the edge of the fairgrounds. Holding her skirt high, Alison plodded upward, along with musicians, guards with fake weapons, and many others.

The queen's yeomen—men on horseback in shining armor—waited at the top of the hill. Nearby sat a gold-painted sedan chair on heavy poles. The queen would ride in it, carried by eight muscular college football players.

Wolfgang came up to the ladies-in-waiting, trumpet in hand. "Alison, did I thank you for saving me from Billy the other day?"

"Only thirty times."

Wolfgang knelt before her. "Make it thirty-one. I'm going to name my first child after you. Matter of fact, I'll name them all after you. I wish—"

"Ladies! Over here, please."

Wolfgang muttered, "Uh-oh, it's Her Maj."

Alison stared at Gwen, astonished at the transformation.

Gwen's plump figure was tightly laced into a high-collared blue gown gleaming with flashy fake jewels. She wore a red wig under her crown. Her face was plastered with pale makeup, and rouge circles adorned her cheeks. The heavy makeup had erased her eyebrows; thin, pencilled arches replaced them. Her lips were painted in a cupid's bow, turned up at the corners in a permanent smile. She seemed to have on a ceramic mask. She looked at Derek, hovering a few feet away.

"It's time," she said, and sat in the sedan chair. The football players lifted her to their shoulders and took their place behind the mounted yeomen. At Derek's signal the musicians struck up a stately march and the procession began to move down the hill. The ladies-in-waiting walked behind the sedan chair, three on either side. Gwen bounced and swayed in the chair. It looked like an uncomfortable ride.

They went through the "village" to the main stage, while customers cheered and vendors and performers removed their hats and bowed. The queen waved and nodded to the left and right.

Twice Alison saw Gwen glare venomously, though her painted smile hid it from most onlookers. The first time was when they passed Robin in the middle of his act. Instead of bowing, he salaamed, dropping to his knees, raising his hands over his head, and bending down until his hands and face were in the dirt. Gwen didn't like it, or the laughs it drew. She also glared when workers in a pottery booth, busy with customers, didn't bow.

On stage, Gwen sat on a throne, flanked by her ladies-in-waiting. After a speech of welcome from Zach, a show was put on for her—and a thousand spectators. The dancers Alison had seen rehearse were first, followed by acrobats and comic actors. Alison didn't like the comics, who did little but scream and do pratfalls, but she applauded anyway.

The show over, the procession exited behind a large curtain hung to conceal the backstage area from the eyes of the public. As Gwen stepped out of her chair, Alison smiled at her.

"That was really—" she began.

"Derek!" The anger in Gwen's voice made Alison jump. "Get over here! *Now!*"

He came forward, looking anxious.

"Yes?" Derek said.

"Sabrina!" Gwendolyn snapped her fingers. "Find Elissa and get her at once."

"Yes, Your Majesty." Sabrina hurried away.

Gwendolyn took a deep breath before addressing Derek. "Was that idiotic comedy group your idea of royal entertainment? They don't belong on the main stage—or on *any* stage. Keep them out of my sight."

Derek squirmed. "In a more intimate setting—"

Gwen snorted. "You have no taste or judgment."

Seeing Elissa heading toward them, Alison said, "Your Maj—"

"Keep quiet, you!" Gwendolyn's voice cut like a whip. "How dare you interrupt!"

Alison was speechless. She pointed wordlessly to Elissa.

"There you are," Gwendolyn said, stepping forward to meet her. "That awful boy is intolerable. I want him dealt with immediately!"

Elissa was calm. "I assume you mean Robin."

"Who else? And some pottery sellers ignored me completely. Make an example of them."

"Calm down, Gwen," urged Elissa. "We'll have a word with the craftspeople. As for Robin—"

"Fire him!" snapped Gwendolyn.

"Can we talk in private?" Elissa asked Gwen.

"No!" Gwen's strident voice turned heads all over the tent, but she didn't seem to care. "You have no control over anything! I heard about that horrid effigy! I'm not Queen Elizabeth anymore, I'm just a woman in costume! Merrie Olde England is becoming a farce!"

"Gwen," replied Elissa, "we get more successful each year. Robin draws crowds and sells tickets, even if he is headstrong—"

"Selling tickets! That's all you care about!" Gwen began pacing angrily. "You compromise the idea of recreating a true old English village, of going back to a simpler, better time, just to make money. . . ."

Behind Alison, Derek murmured, "Soft ice cream."

"If it were up to me—" Gwen said.

"Gwen." Elissa didn't shout, but Gwen stopped. "As I've said—authenticity is *not* what we're about. I don't care about being totally faithful to history as long as we give people fun and value for their money. That's my priority. I'll deal with Robin."

As Elissa walked away, Gwen took Derek's arm and pulled him aside, whispering urgently. Sabrina beckoned to the other girls, who joined her in a hushed group.

"Well, that's over," Bonnie muttered. "Could've been worse, I guess."

"Worse?" echoed Alison. "Are you serious?"

Maxine rolled her eyes. "Once last year, she—" She saw Alison's alarmed expression and stopped. "We'll tell horror stories another time. We have two hours before the Queen's Pageant. Who's hungry?"

Alison wasn't, but she wanted company. The girls changed into street clothes and went to find some lunch.

A while later, they sat under an oak tree after feasting on barbecued chicken and lemonade, paid for with food coupons they got along with their salary.

"What did Robin do to Gwen?" Kayla asked.

Alison explained.

"Boy, Gwen sure has a short fuse," said Tiffany Welles. "Hey, does Robin have a girlfriend? He's awesomely cute."

"Not that I know of," Bonnie replied. "But it doesn't matter. He's after Alison."

She and Maxine grinned at each other, and Alison felt herself turning red.

"No way," she protested.

"He sure looked interested this morning," said Maxine. "Lots of girls would trade places with you. He's good-looking and funny. Check out his act—"

"Sssh! Here he comes," Kayla broke in.

Alison looked over her shoulder to see Robin

approaching, smiling at them . . . well, at her. "Hi. Can I sit down?" He sat next to Alison. "I hear Her Maj threw a fit that registered 4.8 on the Richter scale."

"Why do you do stuff like that to her?" Alison asked. "You know it drives her up the wall."

"Right," agreed Sabrina. "And then other people have to take the heat . . . like us, for instance."

Robin looked Alison up and down. "I don't see any bruises."

"Here you are, Robin." Elissa stood in front of the group, looking grim. Behind her waited a sullen Billy, arms folded. "I've been looking for you."

"Oooh." Robin put his arms over his head. "I'm gonna get spanked."

"Watch it, wise guy," Billy growled.

Elissa's lips tightened. "Can't you be respectful to Gwen? It complicates my life when you're not."

Robin sighed. "She's such a great target . . . but okay, I'll cut it out."

"I'd appreciate it." Elissa smiled. "Alison, I see your dress didn't suffer any damage this morning."

"No, it's fine."

"Funny it was *her* dress, don't you think?" said Billy. He stared down at her, face expressionless.

Robin stood up. "What's that supposed to mean?"

Billy turned to Elissa. "Alison and Robin could've pulled that stunt this morning."

"That's ridiculous!" Alison was furious. She knew from the smirk on Billy's face that he was paying her back for helping Robin in the tent the other day.

"Are you really as stupid as you sound?" Robin planted himself in front of the security man.

"Stop it!" snapped Elissa. "Billy, go about your business. Now."

Billy stomped off. "I'm tired of being a peacemaker all the time," Elissa said.

"Hey, that wasn't my fault," Robin protested.

"I know." Elissa sounded tired as she turned to go. But she was blocked by Eric Sinclair. He stood in her path with a stocky, glowering man in a flashy, open-collared shirt.

"Elissa!" Sinclair greeted her. "Good to see everything going well! I hope it keeps up. Meet my friend, Mr. Tresh."

Mr. Tresh nodded.

"How do you do, Mr. Tresh. Excuse me, please." Elissa stepped around them and walked away.

"See you around, Elissa," Sinclair called. Tresh chuckled hoarsely, as if Sinclair had said something funny. The men drifted down the path.

"Mr. Tresh gives me the creeps," said Kayla.

"What's with that guy Sinclair?" Alison wondered.

Robin said, "He's a builder who wants to develop this land. He keeps offering Elissa big bucks, which she keeps turning down." He pulled a watch out of a leather belt pouch. "Whoa, show time! Alison, want to watch?"

"Go ahead, you've got time," Sabrina urged. "We'll meet you at the tent later."

"Okay," Alison said. "But if you're not funny, don't expect me to laugh."

"Boo and hiss, if you want." He walked her to where two paths crossed and indicated a vacant hay bale. "There you go, a front row seat. Wait a second."

He ran to a nearby booth where a man was selling fruit ices, and brought back a canvas bag. Putting it down, he squatted to rummage through the contents. "Let's see . . ." He pulled out a hat, three knives with long, nasty blades, some rubber balls, three cigar boxes taped shut and painted in bright colors, a battered bugle, and a shiny red apple.

"Watch my gear," he told Alison. "Don't let anyone touch anything, okay? Especially the apple."

He took the bugle and blew a loud ugly blast, making everyone nearby look to see where the hideous noise had come from.

Putting down the bugle, he spread his arms wide. "Lords and ladies, youngsters and oldsters, your attention please! Come one, come all, prepare to be amused and amazed!" A crowd of spectators quickly gathered.

"Robin Goodfellow at your service—jester, juggler, master acrobat, and Merrie Olde England's most marvelous madcap! I'm low in calories, vitamin-rich, need no batteries or subtitles, and I'm good for the environment!"

He began juggling four rubber balls, talking all the while. "Last year, the queen stopped by for a few words. I didn't understand any of them. The lord mayor told me he admired my juggling and fast talking. I said, 'That's high praise, coming from a politician.'"

Alison joined in the laughter. She marveled as Robin switched from rubber balls to cigar boxes, increasing the level of skill required with each stunt. Then he picked up the knives. "Will I lose any fingers today?" he asked, brandishing them. They were long and looked dangerous. "Yes, folks, the blades are real, but don't worry—I have spare hands in my bag." As onlookers gasped, Robin sent the knives in flashing arcs with no mishaps. He did some tumbling—cartwheels, backflips, handstands—before picking up and juggling two rubber balls and the apple.

"Juggling really works up an appetite," he said, snatching and biting into the apple before tossing it up again. He ate the apple down to the core while continuing to juggle it. The crowd, which had grown to a hundred or more, gave him a big round of applause.

He bowed and grabbed the hat from in front of Alison's feet. "All donations gratefully received," he said, extending the hat to his audience. Coins and some bills were put in. "Thanks for your generosity. Enjoy the rest of your day."

The crowd broke up, and Robin stuffed his props back in the bag. He grinned at Alison. "That's that. Want some lemon ice? It's really good."

"Sure. Thanks. You're really good, too."

Robin, who had started toward the fruit-ice

booth, stopped and turned back. "Really? You mean that?"

"Why look surprised? You say it yourself."

He looked away. "I guess I was afraid you wouldn't like the show. I really wanted you to."

This was a new side to Robin. Maybe he wasn't so cocky after all. Alison was startled at the sudden warmth she felt for him.

"I did like it. You're almost as good as you say you are."

Robin laughed. "Just for that, you get two scoops instead of one. Come on."

The ices were the perfect refreshment on a hot day. Alison and Robin sat in a shady spot to enjoy them.

"How did you get into juggling?" Alison asked.

Robin lay back in the grass. "I saw a juggler when I was six. The guy's hands hardly moved, and all those balls and clubs flew around . . . The next day, I started teaching myself. I've been juggling ever since."

They talked on. Alison told Robin how she missed her old friends, and about her family's adjustment problems.

"Finding MOE was a break. I've met neat people and stopped thinking about how boring my life is," Alison said.

"I've met some neat people lately, myself." He gave her a quick sideways glance.

Before Alison could think of what to say to that, she heard her name being called. It was Kayla.

She stood and waved. "Over here!"

Kayla rushed up, panting. "Come on, the Queen's Pageant starts in fifteen minutes!"

Alison felt a stab of panic. She didn't want to make Gwen angry. She turned to Robin.

"Um, thanks, I—"

"Yeah," Robin said. "Better get going."

With Kayla's help, Alison quickly dressed, and the girls hurried up the hill. Gwen waited impatiently.

"It's high time you two got here," she said. The sedan chair was brought over, but she shook her head. "I'll walk."

"Walk?" Alison whispered to Sabrina.

The older girl nodded. "Once in a while, she walks so she can stop and talk to customers. She says it gives them a thrill." Sabrina rolled her eyes.

MOE's biggest spectacle was led by guards in armor, followed by flag bearers. The mounted men came next, then the queen and her ladies. After them came the lord mayor and other MOE officials, along with craftspeople who would display their wares from the main stage. There were guest celebrities dressed in Elizabethan costume. Her Majesty's Wind Ensemble provided music. Last came street performers—tumblers, jesters, clowns. More guards brought up the rear.

The crowd was huge; Billy and his men had to work hard to keep them off the route. The pottery makers who had ignored Gwen before now bowed and cheered with everyone else.

Walking alongside Gwen, Alison let her mind drift to thoughts of Robin. Maybe he did like her.

He cared about what she thought of him, anyway. What were her feelings toward him? He could be a pain, but still . . .

She was jolted from her daydream by a shrill whinny. A few feet away, a horse reared, its rider tugging at the reins. People scattered as the horse bucked and threw the man off. There was sudden confusion as people fought to get away from the maddened horse. In the scramble, someone bumped Alison and knocked her to the ground.

Dazed, she looked up—right at the hooves of the frightened, rearing horse. She froze, unable to move. Then someone pulled her clear and lifted her to her feet. She turned to find a concerned Zach Connors.

"Thanks!" she gasped. "That was—"

"Stay right here," he said, watching the panicky horse, which was still resisting efforts to control it.

A figure darted from the crowd and reached up to stroke the horse's neck, talking gently into its ear. It was Robin. Slowly, the animal grew calm.

"I don't get it," the rider said, dusting himself off. "He's never done anything like that before."

"He'll be okay now." Robin frowned and examined the horse's hindquarters. Then he came over to Alison. "Are you all right?"

Alison mostly felt numb. "I—I guess so. Where'd you learn about horses?"

"On my uncle's ranch in Arizona." He lowered his voice. "There's something weird going on."

"What do you mean?" Alison asked.

"I think someone spooked that horse

deliberately. There was a little drop of blood on its flank."

"Maybe a fly bit it," Alison suggested.

"It didn't look like a horsefly bite—I've seen those. This was more like a pinprick."

Alison stared at him. "Why? Why would anyone deliberately hurt a horse?"

"To cause a scene during the biggest event of the day, in the middle of the biggest crowd. Remember that little prank this morning?"

She recalled the effigy. "You think there's a connection?"

Robin shrugged. "It could be a coincidence, I guess. But if it isn't, then someone may be out to ruin this fair . . . someone who doesn't mind if people get hurt."

5

Order was finally restored, and the pageant resumed. Afterward, Kayla and Alison left to stroll the grounds until Mr. and Mrs. Martínez were ready to leave, while Gwen angrily demanded to know who was responsible for the behavior of the troublesome horse.

As they walked around, Alison told Kayla about Robin's suspicions. Kayla frowned, puzzled.

"Why? Who would want to ruin MOE?"

Alison stopped short, her eyes wide. "Eric Sinclair! With MOE out of the way, he could get this land."

"Hey, yeah!" Kayla said. "Remember what he said to Elissa—that some people aren't as nice as he is? And that Mr. Tresh looked like a real goon to me."

Alison thought for a moment, and sighed. "Yeah, but how about that effigy? They wouldn't know where to get my dress or the crown."

Kayla nodded. "Only insiders would know. So, if the ones who spooked the horse made the effigy, they work here. But if MOE goes, they're out of a job!"

"Who's out of a job?" asked Robin, coming up behind them. "Not me, I hope. I need the money."

Alison explained their suspicions about Eric Sinclair and Mr. Tresh.

Robin nodded. "Sinclair has a motive, for sure."

"But he couldn't have made the effigy," Alison pointed out.

Robin kicked at a wisp of hay. "That's true."

"Have you told anyone what you think about the horse?" asked Kayla.

Robin laughed. "Who would I tell? Everyone thinks I'm a flake. Billy wouldn't believe me if I said the sun would rise in the east tomorrow." He looked around. "I'd hate to see this place become just another mall. I like MOE. If it fails, a lot of people will get hurt."

"Like my folks," Kayla added, her face glum.

"Let's watch out for 'accidents,'" said Alison. "If they keep happening, that proves someone is out to get MOE."

"And what do we do then?" Kayla asked.

Alison wished she knew. "Tell someone, I guess. Meanwhile, we can look around and ask questions."

Robin's eyes widened. "Whoa, time out. Are you saying you want to play detective?"

Put that way, it sounded silly. "All I mean," said Alison, "is we can see what else happens."

Robin ran a hand through his shaggy hair, considering the idea. "I don't know. If we're right, whoever's doing this won't like us snooping around."

"If we find something suspicious," said Alison, "we'll tell Elissa. What risk is there in that?"

"Let's talk about it tomorrow," suggested Kayla.

"Okay, tomorrow," Alison said grumpily.

"Chill out, Sherlock," urged Robin.

"I *said* okay, didn't I?"

"Let's go to Sherwood Forest," said Robin. "You can pretend you're shooting arrows at the creeps who made the effigy. Do you know how?"

Irritated, Alison snapped, "Yes, I know how. I used to do it all the time at camp. I was pretty good. In fact, I might even be better than you are."

Robin's grin had never been more smug and annoying. "Yeah? Okay, Wonder Woman, let's go."

Sherwood Forest, MOE's archery range, was enclosed by a fence and lay some distance from the main grounds. Targets were set up fifty to a hundred yards away from the archers.

The trio arrived to find customers waiting for workers in green costumes to gather arrows from the targets and ground. A large sign in front of the waiting archers read DON'T SHOOT! in huge letters.

"Butch!" called Robin.

A skinny blond boy looked up from a bow he was stringing. "Robin! What ho?"

"Alison here says she's an archery ace. Give her a bow and let her try her hand."

Butch looked her up and down. "Okay," he said at last. "I've got just the bow for you." He handed her the bow he'd just strung, giving Robin a look she couldn't figure out. "Here are some arrows," he said, passing her a bundle of them. The feathered shafts were about two and a half feet long, with needle-sharp metal points.

Butch pointed to a target fifty yards away. "Try this for starters. Want an armguard?" He held out a leather contraption covered with straps and buckles.

Alison shook her head. "That's okay."

"If you say so," said Butch, glancing at Robin again.

"Keep your left arm straight and steady," said Robin softly from behind her. "Make sure your right elbow is—"

"Hey," said Alison. "I can do it, okay?"

He backed off. "Be my guest."

But when Alison notched an arrow and attempted to draw back the bowstring, she was unpleasantly surprised. It was much stiffer than what she'd used at camp. Alison tried to recall the archery counselor's lessons, knowing that Robin and Kayla and Butch were watching.

Her left arm wobbled and the string dug into her fingers. Gritting her teeth, Alison yanked the string back, released it—and yelped in pain as the bowstring raked her unprotected forearm. The arrow fluttered to the ground, halfway to the target. Alison wanted to crawl into a hole and disappear.

Robin hurried forward. "You're rusty, that's all. I wasn't any better my first time."

Butch came over. "Want to try again with an armguard?"

Alison's arm burned, and so did her face—with embarrassment. "No, thanks," she said.

She saw Butch smirking, and angrily realized that she'd been had. Butch must have given her an extra-strong bow, as a little joke at her expense.

But Alison didn't let her anger show. She just handed back the bow and walked away. She was determined to come back and wipe the grin off Butch's face—and show Robin she could do it.

"You okay?" Mrs. Martínez asked Alison on the way to the fair the next day, Sunday. "You look a little down."

"I'm okay," Alison muttered, slumped in the back seat. "I just wish I could say the same for my family."

"Anybody sick over there?" asked Mr. Martínez.

"No, just grouchy. It gets so depressing. Dana whines about everything, and Mom gets on her case for whining, and Dad says Mom isn't understanding enough, and—I couldn't wait to leave."

"It's lucky you have MOE," said Mr. Martínez.

"Yeah. If I hadn't met Kayla . . ."

"If you hadn't met new friends and found something to do," Mrs. Martínez continued gently, "you'd be in the same boat as your family— unhappy and trying to adjust."

"I know," sighed Alison. "I should try to give them some slack. But it's not easy."

"Get them to come out next weekend," Kayla urged.

"It won't be easy, especially Dana—but maybe."

"I almost forgot," said Kayla. "You remember the thing with the horse yesterday? My aunt saw it on the TV news."

Alison stared at her. "You're kidding!"

"Someone got it on video," said Mr. Martínez. "They showed a woman who sprained her ankle and Elissa saying they'd never had problems with the horses before."

"They treated it like a joke," Mrs. Martínez said.

"That 'joke' can scare off customers," said her husband.

Alison remembered Robin's words: Someone wanted to cause an ugly scene during MOE's biggest event, in the middle of the biggest crowd. Maybe it wasn't chance that it got on the news. Maybe the people who spooked the horse had also sent the video to the TV station.

It was going to be a hot day, Alison thought, as she and Kayla entered the performers' tent. They were greeted by Gwen's angry voice. She stood in full costume and makeup, shouting at an unhappy Derek.

"What's happening?" Kayla asked a grim-faced Bonnie.

"Elissa decided not to use the horses any more. You know yesterday's accident was on TV last night?"

Kayla and Alison nodded.

"Anyway," Bonnie continued, "Derek told

Gwen and she went ballistic. Better keep your distance."

Maxine came in, heard Gwen, and stopped in her tracks. The others told her what was happening.

"Let's wait here for a bit," Maxine suggested. "Maybe she'll get tired, or get laryngitis or something."

At that moment, Gwen saw the huddle of girls. "Why are you dawdling around like that?" she demanded, her voice shrill. "Why aren't you dressed?"

No one answered.

Gwen threw up her hands. "I'm surrounded by morons!" She turned back to find that Derek, seeing his chance, had escaped from the tent. That made her even madder. She strode over to the girls. "Do we pay you to stand around like store-window dummies? Get dressed! If anyone's late for the procession, they're fired! *Go!*"

With their eyes averted from Gwen's flushed face, the girls headed for the makeup area. Sabrina and Tiffany were already there, applying eye shadow at adjoining mirrors.

"Hi," said Tiffany, her voice low. "Her Maj is at it again. Was the real Queen Elizabeth like this?"

Sabrina looked around. "Gwen loved having horses in the procession. She'll get over it eventually."

Kayla cautiously peered around the tent. "Good. She's talking to Zach," she reported. "Let's duck into the changing room while she's not looking our way."

As she got her dress, Alison heard Zach's powerful voice ring out. She peeked out of the changing room.

Towering over Gwen, the lord mayor was giving her an earful. "Listen, lady, don't scream at me! I won't stand for it! Back here, you're just an employee like everyone else, so save your act for the customers."

Zach walked away, eyes blazing, leaving Gwen blinking and speechless in his wake. Alison ducked back into the changing room before Gwen could see her. Interesting, she thought. Zach stood up to Gwen, and she backed down. Of course, that's Zach. It wouldn't work if I tried it. But it was good to know that Gwen wasn't all-powerful around here.

Possibly because of her brush with Zach, Gwen refrained from further outbursts that morning. Alison thought the procession looked fine without mounted men. Instead of horses, there were additional flags and banners.

At one point in the parade, Kayla nudged her, and gestured toward the crowd. Eric Sinclair and Mr. Tresh stood by the path, watching. Sinclair wore a short-sleeved knit shirt and slacks, while Tresh sported a loose Hawaiian shirt, gaudy with flowers. Unlike the rest of the crowd, they didn't clap or cheer or smile. Why were they back?

The sun stood high in a cloudless sky when the procession left the main stage. Alison was eager to put on street clothes for a while. The bare wooden stage was like a giant sun reflector, adding ten or fifteen degrees to the hot day. How did Gwen stand it in that makeup and costume?

"Lunchtime!" Sabrina called out.

"I don't much care what I eat," said Bonnie, "but I want a gallon of ice-cold lemonade."

The others agreed. Once out of costume, they made a beeline for the nearest cold drink booth. With a last-second sprint, Kayla got there first.

"Lemonade, please. The biggest one you have."

"Sorry, we don't have any," said the woman behind the counter. Alison noticed that the booth was doing very little business, despite the heat.

Kayla gaped. "You're kidding! Why?"

The woman looked nervous. "We ran out. Sorry."

The girls exchanged looks of dismay. Tiffany said, "How could you run out of lemonade by noon?"

"I . . . look, we don't have any, that's all. There's cider and ginger beer."

Everyone settled for cider. As they left, Sabrina asked, "What was that all about?"

Alison sipped from her cup. "Why weren't there a lot of customers? The place was empty."

"Anybody hungry?" asked Maxine.

They bought falafels and looked for a shady place to sit. That took a while, since a lot of people wanted to stay out of the sun.

"What ho, ladies! Hot enough for you?" Wolfgang flopped in the grass beside them, wiping his face with a bandanna. "You can fry eggs on the stage. Or musicians." He waved to someone behind Alison. Turning, she felt a sudden surge of happiness when she saw Robin approaching.

"Hi!" she called. "Join the party!"

He looked more serious than usual.

"What's up?" she asked. "Heat getting to you?"

His smile sent a rush of warmth through her. "This is nothing. Wait till it's really hot, when the sun bakes the stage so actors can't lie down for death scenes—they have to die standing up or sitting in a chair. They sprinkle the stage with water—"

"—and it turns to steam," said Wolfgang. "Last year one musician melted completely. All that was left was his costume, lying in a pool of water."

"Alison, can I talk to you in private?" Robin asked.

Alison saw grins on the other girls' faces.

"Don't let us keep you," said Bonnie.

"He wants to know if you've read any good books lately," joked Maxine.

Alison stood up. "See you guys later."

"Don't lose track of the time," warned Sabrina. "You definitely don't want to cross Gwen today."

"I'll be there," promised Alison. She could sense the girls' eyes on them as she walked away with Robin.

They strolled past a small crowd being entertained by a pair of mimes. "What's wrong?" she asked.

"Have you tried to get lemonade lately?" he asked.

"A while ago. They said they didn't have any."

Robin nodded. "Right now a dozen people are in the infirmary with stomach pains. I heard they'll be okay, but at the moment they're pretty sick. It seems they all drank lemonade from that booth."

He pointed to where the girls had been earlier. "Billy's boys took the bottled lemonade concentrate from the booths to get it tested for contamination. Meanwhile, there's no lemonade until further notice."

Stunned, Alison stared at Robin. "Yesterday, a horse went crazy, which never happened here before. Now, something's wrong with the lemonade."

"Uh-huh," said Robin. "They're not sloppy or careless handling food and drinks here, either."

"Did you know that the business with the horse made the TV news last night?" asked Alison.

Robin's eyes widened. "Really?" He looked grim. "I think it's time to talk to Elissa. I have time before my next show. I just hope she hears me out."

"I'll go with you," said Alison.

"I hoped you would," Robin said, reaching out a hand. After a moment, Alison took it in her own. There was wiry strength in his fingers, but his grip was gentle. "Come on, let's check her office."

Robin led her toward a small stucco building near the main gate, where MOE's offices were located.

"There she is!" exclaimed Alison. Elissa and Derek stood talking by the front door. Elissa's face was haggard, as though she hadn't gotten much sleep. She looked up as they came over.

"I'm busy right now. If it's not important . . ."

"Actually, it is," said Robin. Derek tapped a foot, looking impatient.

"We heard about the lemonade," Robin went on, quickly. "We think it's part of a plot to sabotage MOE—I mean the fair."

He explained his theory about the horse.

"Maybe the people who spooked the horse also made sure that it was videotaped," added Alison. "And then they sent the tape to the TV station, so that customers would think twice about coming here. Remember, that effigy had a sign saying WATCH OUT. They want to scare us as well as the customers."

Elissa and Derek listened without interrupting. At least they're paying attention, Alison thought.

"Who would do such a thing?" Derek demanded.

"It could be Eric Sinclair," suggested Robin. "He'd love to get you off this land."

"He's back today," said Alison. "Along with that Mr. Tresh, whoever he is."

Elissa frowned. "He's here again?"

"Uh-huh," Alison replied. "I saw them."

"He'd be capable of sabotage," said Derek.

"You did the right thing, coming to me," Elissa said. "But let's keep it to ourselves."

Alison nodded. "What are you going to do?"

"I'm not sure yet," replied Elissa. "Right now, I have to meet a crew from Channel 8. They're going to shoot the fair for tonight's news. Maybe we'll get some good publicity for a change. If there's anything else I should know about, please tell me or Derek."

Derek nodded. "I never did like Sinclair."

"How long till your next show?" Alison asked, as she and Robin walked back from the office.

"I've got some time. What about you? We don't want Her Maj to have another fit."

"I have almost an hour yet."

"Let's find Sinclair and Tresh," Robin said. "Maybe we can keep an eye on them."

They walked through the fair without spotting the men. Alison saw Sabrina and Maxine sitting under a tree. She grabbed Robin's hand and pulled him over to them.

Sabrina smiled. "Back already? I didn't expect you till five minutes before the pageant."

"Have you seen Sinclair or Tresh?" Robin asked.

"Tresh?" echoed Maxine. "The creepy-looking guy in the hideous shirt? I think I saw them headed toward Sherwood Forest a while ago."

"Thanks!" Alison turned to leave.

"Don't be late!" called Sabrina.

But Sinclair and Tresh weren't at the archery range when Alison and Robin arrived. Butch came over, looking sheepish. "Hi. How's your arm?"

"It's okay." Alison put a chill into her voice. "Since we're here, let me try my luck again. This time, I want an armguard . . . and a bow that someone besides Arnold Schwarzenegger could use."

Butch reddened. "I thought you'd just give up without . . . I didn't figure you'd really try to shoot with that bow. It was a pretty stupid trick, I guess."

Alison nodded. "You're right, it was."

"Hey, I'm sorry. Really. Wait a sec." Butch walked away and got a bow, arrows, and an armguard. "This should do it."

She tried the bow, which bent easily.

Butch grinned. "No hard feelings?"

Alison didn't grin back. "Just don't turn your back on me while I've got a bow and arrow handy."

Properly equipped, Alison soon bunched her last several arrows tightly in the target. Two were bull's-eyes. Robin applauded.

"You'd give me some real competition," he said.

Alison swung around to face him. "Surprised? Grab a bow. I bet I can outshoot you."

He pulled his watch from the pouch on his belt. "Sorry, it's almost show time. Gotta go earn some money. We'll do it another time, okay?"

Alison stared at him, hands on hips. "What's the matter, scared you might get beaten by a girl?"

"Who, me?" Robin placed a hand over his heart. "I promise, we'll have a shootout sometime soon, and may the best man—uh, person—win. Shake on it?"

She reached out a hand, and he took it in both of his. They stood like that, not moving, looking into each others' eyes. For Alison, time seemed to stop. The sights and sounds of MOE faded until there was nothing and no one except her and Robin.

After an endless moment, Robin took a deep breath and released her hand. The world rushed back. "We'd better go," he said quietly.

Returning Alison's gear, they walked down the path through the woods, taking their time, reluctant to break the spell that had fallen over them. Alison's mind was swirling with unspoken feelings. Robin didn't say anything, but she sensed that he, too, was trying to come to terms with his emotions.

As they reached the end of the cool, dim path, they saw a crowd of people gathered a few yards away.

From the confused babble of voices, Alison heard a shout: "Please, everyone, move back! Give him air!"

"Is there a doctor here?" yelled someone else.

Alarmed, they headed toward the people. A woman called, "Let me through! I'm a doctor."

As the crowd parted to let the woman through, Alison saw a man lying on his back on the dusty ground. His skin was pale, his eyes shut. He didn't move.

Sticking out of his left thigh was the feathered shaft of an arrow.

"What happened?" Alison asked a woman nearby.

Shaken, the woman clutched the hand of a little boy who was too young to grasp what had happened.

"He was right in front of us! He just grabbed his leg and fell! That arrow could have hit my child!"

"Did you see where it came from?" Robin asked.

"From those trees," said a man, pointing to the woods by the path to Sherwood Forest. "They're crazy to use real arrows here. Someone could be killed."

Several other onlookers nodded, looking upset.

"It's really safe," said Alison. "The archery range is way on the other side of the woods, and there's a fence—"

"Yeah, right!" said the man. "You won't catch me coming here again!"

"What's going on?" Billy Hawley ran up and took in the scene. He stared at Alison and Robin.

The doctor said, "I don't think it's too bad—the arrow missed the major blood vessels, luckily. But he's in shock. We need a stretcher and an ambulance."

Billy spoke into his walkie-talkie. "They're on the way," he said. "What happened?" he asked Robin.

"We didn't see anything," Robin replied. "When we got here, the guy was already on the ground."

"The arrow came from those trees," said Alison, pointing.

Billy nodded. "Uh-huh. And right after that, you two turn up. Where were you?"

"Sherwood Forest. I wanted to . . ." Alison faltered for a moment. "I wanted to try some target practice."

Billy gave her a nasty smile. "I bet you did."

Several security guards ran up, carrying a stretcher. Quickly, the wounded man was taken to wait for the ambulance at the front gate.

"The rest of you," Billy ordered his men, "check the woods where the arrow came from and see what you can find."

Among the gawkers, Alison saw a TV crew, shooting the whole scene. Elissa stood by, looking stricken. MOE wouldn't get good publicity on TV that night.

As the crowd dispersed, Billy focused on Robin and Alison. "So," he said, his voice soft, "you were playing Robin Hood and an arrow got loose and hit a customer. Isn't that right?"

"It's totally wrong," snapped Robin.

A security man emerged from the trees, holding a bow by the string. "We just found this."

Billy nodded. "Look familiar?" he asked Robin.

Robin turned away, looking furious. "I've had enough of this garbage. I have a show to do."

Billy reached out and spun him around by the shoulder. "I'm not done with you yet."

Robin lashed out, knocking Billy's hand away.

"Stop it!" Elissa stepped between them, her voice an urgent whisper. "There's a TV crew here! Hasn't there been enough damage already this weekend? Do you want to put another nail in our coffin?"

Robin's anger could barely be contained. "He says I shot that guy! Mr. Security here would rather get me in trouble than try to find out who really did it."

Billy was just as mad. "It's just the kind of stupid, wiseguy stunt that a punk like you would pull!"

"It wasn't Robin!" Alison insisted. "I was with him the whole time!"

"Wonderful," sneered Billy. "You cover for him and he covers for you. Very convincing."

"Elissa," said Robin. "I may have done stupid things . . . okay, I've definitely done stupid things. But I'd never risk hurting anyone."

"Billy," said Elissa. "You handled the situation with the wounded man beautifully. Thank you."

Billy shrugged. "Just doing my job, that's all."

"But your feelings about Robin are affecting your judgment. I don't believe he'd be that reckless."

A flush crept up Billy's neck. "But—"

"Billy, please. Meet me in my office in a few minutes. I have to go over some things with you."

Billy muttered under his breath, and stomped off.

"Now," Elissa said. "Let's all get back to work."

"I almost forgot!" Robin exclaimed. "The reason we went to Sherwood Forest was that Sinclair and Tresh had gone that way a little while before."

"Right!" Alison said. "Maybe Butch saw them."

"I'll have Billy look into it," answered Elissa. Seeing a scornful look on Robin's face, she went on. "Don't start with me, Robin. Billy's good at his job. Now, you have a show to do, and Alison, you'd better run if you don't want to miss the Queen's Pageant."

Alison looked at her watch. "Oh, no!" She had just enough time to make it, if she ran. She ran.

"See you later," Robin shouted as she raced away.

With the other girls' help, Alison hurried into her dress and makeup. They got to the top of the hill just before Gwen climbed into her sedan chair. As they started down, Kayla leaned toward Alison.

"Kaye and Larry are showing their crafts on stage today," she whispered.

Alison whispered back, "Robin and I saw another 'accident.' I'll tell you later."

"Another one? What—"

"If you two find that these pageants interfere with your gabfests," snarled Gwen from her chair, "we can make other arrangements."

The girls were silent.

It seemed to Alison that fewer people watched the parade than on the previous day, and the mood was definitely less festive. Among the spectators she spotted Sinclair and Tresh. Tresh muttered in Sinclair's ear, and Sinclair laughed.

Kaye and Larry were the last craftspeople Zach called to show the queen their wares. The others had done much bowing and scraping, delighting Gwen. But Larry, though happy to let the crowd see the products of Kayla Krafts, wouldn't play the game. In place of a bow, he gave only a barely noticeable bob of the head. After they had shown their handsome bags and belts, he waved to the crowd, and repeated the little head bob as he left the stage. Gwen's face was angry under the painted smile.

They barely reached the tent before Gwen erupted. "How dare they treat me like that?" she screamed. "I want those boors kicked out! Those miserable little leathermongers should be on their knees, thanking me for the chance to display their trash!"

"Hey!" said Kayla, ignoring frantic signals from Sabrina and Bonnie, "you're trashing my parents!"

Gwen glared at the girl. "The apple doesn't fall far from the tree! I see where you get your lack of breeding—pushing yourself forward as a lady-in-waiting, jabbering during the procession . . . you're your parents' child, all right!"

"And I'm proud to be their child!" Kayla yelled, furious and upset. "You have no right . . . they're the best parents that anyone ever . . . you're just a . . ."

She burst into tears and ran into the changing room. Alison and Bonnie followed.

They found Kayla sobbing in one corner. Alison put her arms around her friend.

"I don't care!" Kayla gasped between sobs. "Let them fire me! She's a horrible witch!"

Bonnie took her hands. "You have a lot of guts, facing up to her like that. Way to go."

Slowly, Kayla's crying subsided. The other girls came in and clustered around them.

Tiffany was pale and angry. "What she did was unbelievable, even for Gwen."

Sabrina put an arm around Kayla's shoulders. "Gwen stormed out to find Elissa and demand that your folks be kicked out. Better warn them."

"I'll come with you," Alison offered.

"Thanks, but you don't have to. I'm fine."

The two girls changed as fast as they could, and left the tent together. Robin was waiting just outside.

"I've got a show in ten minutes. Want to watch?"

"I have to pass," Kayla replied. "Alison, I'll meet you here later."

The two girls hugged, and Kayla ran off.

"Has she been crying?" Robin asked.

As they went to get Robin's props, Alison told him what had happened between Gwen and the Martínez family.

"I'll say it before you do," she added. "You told me so. I thought you were just exaggerating."

"She's worse than she used to be. Elissa let her get away with this stuff for years, and now she thinks she can do and say anything. Gwen's not the queen of England, but she thinks she's the queen of MOE."

"Will Elissa fire the Martínezes?"

Robin shook his head. "I hope not. Elissa should remind Gwen who's boss here. But she has a lot on her mind right now, and she may not want to fight that battle."

Robin's show went well. He juggled balls, knives, and flaming torches, with his usual jokes and patter. The applause was loud, and Robin collected a hatful of money. After the show, they stowed his gear at the fruit-ice booth.

Alison said, "Let's go to that grove where you scared me with that awful black and white makeup."

Robin winced. "Don't remind me. I wanted to impress you so much that day."

She took his hand as they walked. "You wanted to impress me? Really?"

"Absolutely. But the harder I tried, the more idiotic I acted. I figured you'd never speak to me again."

It was quiet under the huge trees. Alison sat back against a tree trunk, and Robin lay facing her.

"I almost couldn't watch you juggle today."

Robin stared. "Was I that bad?"

"Bad? You were great! But I'm afraid you'll cut yourself or get burned."

He shook his head. "It's not dangerous. With regular knives, sure, I'd get hurt. But these knives are especially for juggling—the handles are weighted for the right balance, so I never catch the blades. And the torches are dramatic, but I've never been burned. The riskier it looks, the more money I take in."

She smiled. "Pretty clever."

Robin turned over on his back, cradling his head in his arms. "I need money for college. My parents won't be able to pay for everything, the way things are lately."

"How *are* things lately?" asked Alison.

"Dad was laid off from a computer software company last year, and hasn't had steady work since. Then the law office where Mom's a paralegal cut back her hours. This summer I've been cooking burgers at a fast-food place on weekdays, and I work here on weekends."

"It sounds tough," Alison said. "My father was worried he might get laid off because they were talking about shutting the plant down. Is that what happened with your dad?"

"No. He got into a hassle with his supervisor, and the guy found some lame excuse to get rid of him. Dad won't put up with bullies and loudmouths."

"Hmm. Sounds like someone else I know."

Robin rolled over and grinned at her. "Me, you

mean? Sure! You have to stand up to people like Billy Hawley and Her Majesty, or they'll walk all over you."

"I guess," Alison said, though she wasn't sure she agreed. "But Billy can beat you up, and your dad lost his job."

"Dad says nothing's more important than your self-respect. And don't be so sure Billy can beat me up."

Alison took his hand. "He's big and mean. If you say you won't get hurt juggling knives, I believe you. But when I think of you fighting Billy, I get scared."

"When Billy gets on my case, I can't just let it go. I like it that you worry about me." He gave her hand a gentle squeeze.

"Of course I worry," Alison said. "If you get hurt, you'll use it as an excuse to avoid our archery contest. I want you healthy when I beat you."

Robin looked at Alison's watch and groaned. "Four o'clock! I have a show, and then I have to take off. I'm covering for a buddy at the burger place tonight."

"I'll stay here in the shade," said Alison. "So . . . I'll see you next Saturday, then."

"Count on it. Uh . . . can I call you this week?"

"I'd love it. Here's our number."

They stood up reluctantly.

"Bye," he said. "Watch out for those dragons."

"And bears," she murmured.

He leaned forward and his lips softly brushed hers. Alison wished the moment would last forever.

"Well," he said, breaking the silence. "See you."

He walked away, stopping once to look back. Alison watched him go, her heart pounding.

Was this what falling in love was all about? Alison had had crushes before, but this was much more intense. She lay on her stomach, trying to sort it all out. What a mixture Robin was: funny, gifted, proud, gentle, cocky, sweet—

A branch snapped with a crack like a pistol shot. Startled, Alison scrambled to her feet.

She saw no one. Behind her, slow, heavy footsteps crunched through leaves and twigs. Alison spun around.

"Who is it? Is somebody there?"

No one answered. The steps drew closer. She squinted, blinded by the brilliant rays of sun slanting down between the boughs. Through a gap between the trunks of a nearby cluster of trees, she saw a shadowy figure. Was someone stalking her?

Alison turned to run—and tripped on an exposed root. Her head hit the ground hard as she fell.

She lay stunned, face in the dirt, the wind knocked out of her. Footsteps came up and stopped beside her. Then a thin, whispery voice in her ear said, "You and your boyfriend better mind your own business. This is your last warning. Next time, you'll be hurt."

The footsteps walked away, in the direction from which they'd come. A moment later Alison was able to take a breath, sit up, and look around.

She was alone in the trees.

7

Alison got up on rubbery legs and brushed herself off. Blood trickled from a scratch on one knee, but she seemed to be in one piece. Her watch said, incredibly, that just a few minutes had passed since Robin had left to do his show.

Who had threatened her? The whispery voice could have belonged to anyone at all. She'd only seen a shadowy figure behind the trunks of some big trees.

Suddenly, Alison recalled the dream she'd had in this very place, the first day she'd come to MOE. There had been a dark, menacing figure then, too, turning her dream into a nightmare.

But this had definitely not been a dream.

Alison wanted to get out of the trees, back to the reassuring presence of many people. Hurriedly, she started toward the main stage, and felt relief when she got to the edge of the woods. She raced into the open, looking back over her shoulder. No one was there.

Abruptly, she collided with someone.

Turning, she said, "Sorry, I ought to look where I'm—" She stopped in midapology. The person she'd bumped into was Mr. Tresh. Hastily, she stepped back.

Mr. Tresh stared at her. There was something menacing about the burly man in the garish shirt. Why was he here, in an area not open to the public? And where was his usual companion, Eric Sinclair?

"What are you doing here?" The question came out sounding more hostile than Alison had intended.

"Is this place off limits?" The man's voice was raspy and harsh. "I'm waiting for Mr. Sinclair. He's talking to Ms. Yarborough in there." He indicated the performers' tent. "He said to wait here."

Before Alison could respond, Elissa stormed angrily from the tent, with Eric Sinclair on her heels. She spun around to face him. "Enough, Mr. Sinclair! You're not going to wear me down. Now, I have business to attend to."

Alison saw the smile fade from Sinclair's face. "Okay, Elissa. No more games. Forget the price I gave you yesterday. It just got cut in half. Next week it gets halved again. After that . . . well, I probably won't have to give you a cent. You'll be out of business." He strode away, Tresh at his heels.

"Elissa?" Alison asked. "Could MOE really go out of business?" She kicked herself mentally for forgetting Kayla's advice and calling the fair MOE.

Elissa didn't seem to notice. She turned to Alison, smiling. "Pay no attention to Mr. Sinclair. He's just trying to bully me into taking his offer with scare tactics. We're not closing down. This place has weathered storms before, and we'll weather this one, too."

But Alison sensed that, in spite of her brave talk, Elissa was more worried than she'd let on.

During the week the fair was often on the TV news. There were shots of colorful pageantry and costumed performers. But there was also a lot of footage of the rearing, bucking horse, along with tales of customers poisoned by tainted lemonade and wounded by errant arrows. Fair patrons were shown saying that they'd once loved the fair, but wouldn't go back.

Alison hadn't told her folks about the threat in the woods. She knew if they heard about that, they'd forbid her to return. And then she might not see Robin again.

She'd been waiting for him to call. Whenever the phone rang she held her breath, but so far he hadn't been in touch. Alison told herself to relax, that with his weekday job, Robin was very busy. Also, the week wasn't over yet.

On Tuesday night she had dinner with Kayla and her parents. Mr. Martínez turned out to be a fantastic cook and the evening was fun. Kayla would have dinner at the Crisps' two nights later. She told Alison that Elissa had persuaded Mr.

Martínez to bow to the queen whenever a procession came by. As a result Kayla Krafts would stay on at the fair.

On Wednesday Alison and her family saw a TV news report that lab tests had found epsom salts in some of MOE's lemonade concentrate. A doctor came on and said that, while epsom salts weren't deadly when swallowed, they could cause severe stomach pains. It was also announced that Sherwood Forest would be closed until further notice.

Mrs. Crisp looked at Alison with concern. "Ally, is that fair safe? Maybe you should quit."

"Mom, you know they always exaggerate on the news."

Mrs. Crisp didn't look convinced. She started to say something else, but the phone rang and she went to answer it.

"Alison! It's for you!" Alison jumped up and ran to grab the cordless receiver from Mrs. Crisp's outstretched hand.

"Hello?"

"Hi, it's Robin."

"Oh, hi." She tried to sound cool and relaxed, but her insides were churning. She took the phone to the den and shut the door.

"How are you doing?" he asked.

"Good. How are you?"

"Okay. Working. Looking forward to the weekend."

"Me too," she said softly.

"Did Her Maj get the Martínezes kicked out?"

"No," she answered. "Mr. Martínez said he'd behave. And something happened to me after you left Sunday."

She told him about the whispered threat and about bumping into Mr. Tresh immediately afterward.

"Wow! Are you okay?" Alison could hear the concern in Robin's voice. "Were you scared?"

"Definitely, but I'm okay now. I realized that if he'd wanted to hurt me, he could have. We were alone, and I was just lying there. I guess he only wanted to frighten me. He sure did a good job of it."

"Do you think it was Tresh?" asked Robin.

"There's no way to be sure. But he's always nearby when something bad happens. Then, Eric Sinclair told Elissa that MOE would be out of business soon. Elissa looked worried."

"I don't blame her," Robin answered. "Have you been watching the news on TV?"

"Uh-huh. It looks bad, doesn't it?"

"Those news stories are going to scare people away. If attendance drops off a lot, that could put Elissa in a bind. MOE's an expensive show to run."

Alison, who had been sprawled out on the couch, sat up straight. "You mean, if too few people show up, MOE really could be in serious trouble?"

"It could be. If things are bad for a few weekends in a row . . ." Robin's voice trailed off.

"It'd be great to find the proof to nail Sinclair and Tresh, if they're behind this. Let's try to work on it this weekend."

"I'll look forward to it," Robin said. He paused a moment. "And to seeing you again. Which reminds me, on Saturday night there's a red lantern show at seven-thirty."

"What's that?" asked Alison.

"It's done for the people who work at the fair and miss the entertainment during the day. They do two or three every summer and they're always fun. Want to go? I'll bet the Martínezes want to see it, too."

"It sounds great. Sure!"

"Ally! Are you going to hog the phone all night?" Dana was shouting through the closed door of the den. "Daddy said I could call Gina."

Gina was Dana's closest friend in Connecticut.

Alison sighed. "Just a minute!" she yelled. "I have to go," she told Robin. "My dear little sister wants the phone. But I'm glad you called."

"Me, too. See you Saturday. Bye."

"Bye."

She hung up and opened the door. There stood Dana, arms folded, foot tapping, face screwed up in a frown.

"I have to call right now, 'cause it's three hours later in Connecticut. I thought you'd never get off!"

Thinking of Robin, Alison was too happy to snap at her sister. She went out to enjoy the cool evening air. California, she decided, had its good points.

The next night Kayla came for dinner. Earlier that day, Alison had warned her not to alarm Mr.

and Mrs. Crisp with talk of suspicious events at MOE.

"I love this chicken," said Kayla, helping herself to a second drumstick. "Great barbecue sauce! It's even better than the chicken Oscar sells at the fair."

Mrs. Crisp smiled. "Thanks, Kayla. It was sweet of you to ask Ally to go out there with you. I must say, it does sound wonderful—like history brought to life. I just can't help worrying about what I've been seeing on the news . . ."

"Mom—" Alison began. Kayla cut in smoothly.

"It's not as bad as they make it look. You should come out this weekend! Ally looks gorgeous in that gown, and you'd have a great time."

Mr. and Mrs. Crisp exchanged a look. "I've been putting in crazy hours," said Mr. Crisp. "But I'd love to see Ally looking like a princess."

Mrs. Crisp nodded. "We are free this weekend. What do you think, Dana?"

"It sounds like a big yawn," Dana sneered.

"But you'll come see your sister anyway, won't you, kitten?" said Mr. Crisp, with a meaningful look. "Just like Ally always goes to your dance recitals and your school plays, because she's your sister, and she loves you, and she's proud of what you do. Right?"

Dana stared at the wall. "I guess," she muttered.

"There!" Mrs. Crisp beamed at everybody. "It's settled then. We'll come this Saturday or Sunday. Dear, what day do you think would be best?"

Mr. Crisp rubbed both hands over his face, looking tired. "Better make it Sunday. Saturday I might have to put in some time at the office."

The next day, Alison was in her room when her mother appeared in the doorway. "This came for you in the mail." Mrs. Crisp held out a white envelope.

Puzzled, Alison took it. It looked like a birthday or holiday card, but it wasn't anywhere near her birthday or a holiday. She turned the envelope over, but there was no return address.

"Thanks, Mom," she said. Mrs. Crisp nodded and left the room.

Alison tore open the envelope and fished out a glossy, white card bordered in black. The words *Deepest Sympathy* were printed on the front.

She opened the card. The message inside had been hand-printed in bright red block letters:

KEEP YOUR MOUTH SHUT AND MIND YOUR OWN BUSINESS, OR YOUR PARENTS WILL GET A LOT OF THESE CARDS.

"This is not good. Not good at all."

Mr. Martínez drove past MOE's customer parking lot on Saturday morning. Alison and Kayla looked out of the rear windows, and silently agreed with his comment.

The lot, which had been half full by 9:00 A.M. the previous weekend, was mostly empty. Instead of thousands of eager customers waiting to get in, there were just a few hundred. The parking lot attendants, who had raced around last weekend, now lounged with their hands in their pockets and little to do.

"It's the TV news," said Mrs. Martínez. "People are scared of being skewered by an arrow or trampled by a horse—"

"Or poisoned," Mr. Martínez finished. "Great. We'll be lucky to break even today."

"Relax," Mrs. Martínez said. "People have short memories. Next week they'll find something else to shout about, and this will be forgotten."

"Unless something else happens," her husband said darkly. "Then the TV people will get it all. See?"

Four vans sat in the employee parking lot. Each featured the logo of a different TV channel.

"Maybe the crews will buy our things," said Mrs. Martínez. "And there's a red lantern show tonight. That's something to look forward to. Things could be worse."

Mr. Martínez merely grunted as he parked the van. He and his wife began to unload their new wares, while the girls started toward the main stage.

"Kayla!" called her mother. "Remember what we said. Be careful about what you eat and drink!"

"I will, don't worry!" Kayla called back.

Alison observed that the people setting up shop around them were quieter than the week before. "Everyone seems kind of down today," she said.

"You got that right. Hey, hi, Robin!"

"What ho, ladies!" Robin was leaning against a tree, and Alison knew at once that he'd been waiting for her. She felt her face grow warm.

"Hi," she said, feeling strangely shy but, at the same time, very happy.

Robin came over. "Hi. Could we talk a minute?"

Kayla said, "I'll see you in the tent, okay?"

"Sure."

As Kayla walked away, Robin motioned for Alison to sit with him on a hay bale. He reached into his pouch. "Look at this." He pulled out a glossy white card with a black border.

"I got one, too," she said, opening it. The message was identical.

Robin took the card. "It figures." He stood up, looking worried. "Maybe we should back off. People have been hurt already."

"Are you worried about getting hurt?" asked Alison.

"I can take care of myself."

"Then why back off?"

"It's just . . . if anything happened to you, I'd . . ."

Alison was annoyed. "You think I can't take care of myself because I'm a girl?"

Robin persisted. "If you got hurt, I'd feel I'd dragged you into a dangerous situation."

"First of all," Alison said, a chill in her voice, "you didn't drag me. I was the one who said we should snoop around, not you. Second, I'm not a helpless damsel looking for a big, strong man to protect her. If that's the kind of girl you want, keep looking, because you haven't found her yet."

Robin raised his hands in surrender. "Wait! I didn't say you can't . . . well, maybe I did but I didn't mean . . . okay! If you're game, Sherlock, so am I. Deal?"

"Deal," she agreed, smiling. "Walk me to the performers' tent, okay?"

Robin took her hand and Alison's anger melted away. "Are you staying for the red lantern show tonight?"

"Uh-huh. I can get a ride home with the Martínezes." She pointed out a TV crew to Robin. "Look at that."

"I've seen them. They're all over the place."

Near the main stage, Alison was startled by a hand on her shoulder. It was Derek, looking anxious.

"I'd like a word with you," he said. "It won't take long, and it might be important."

Robin shrugged. "Why not?" They went behind the tent for greater privacy.

Derek's eyes darted around, as if he feared being seen. "I'm worried about what's happening here. Did you see the TV crews? And the pitiful crowd waiting to get in? Hardly a crowd; more like a handful."

"We noticed," Alison replied.

"I heard you tell Elissa that you think there's a plan to destroy Merrie Olde England."

"It looks that way," said Robin. "From the number of customers, I'd say the plan is already working."

Derek nodded. "I agree." He looked at Alison. "Elissa and I founded Merrie Olde England twenty years ago. The first one was in Elissa's backyard, and only fifty people came. Now, we employ hundreds; we entertain over a hundred thousand; some vendors make much of their living here; and the richest creative period in history gets an annual tribute. The idea of it being ruined doesn't bear thinking about."

As he talked about MOE, Derek's voice

trembled. He seemed to be on the verge of tears.

"What do you want from us?" she asked.

Derek lowered his voice to a whisper. "I want to team up to stop whoever is causing our problems. We can pool our information, and I'll feel better, knowing I'm fighting to keep Merrie Olde England alive. What do you say?"

Robin looked to Alison for a response. "I guess that makes sense," she said, after a moment's thought.

"Good!" Derek leaned forward. "Tell me—what have you discovered, and who are your suspects?"

They told him about the threats they'd received. "Our main suspects are Eric Sinclair, and his pal, Mr. Tresh," said Robin.

"They pop up in suspicious places," Alison added. "They were seen near the archery range just before that man was wounded with an arrow. I ran into Mr. Tresh a minute after being threatened last week. And they were hanging around here all last Saturday and Sunday."

Derek nodded. "Sinclair is a ruthless, greedy man who'd do anything to get what he wants. Billy says Sinclair and Tresh were loitering here late last Friday, after rehearsals. Maybe that's when they got hold of the queen's crown and your dress for that effigy."

"Do you know anything about Tresh?" Robin asked.

Derek shook his head. "Only that he has horrible taste in shirts and looks like a hired thug."

Alison looked at her watch. "I have to get

ready for the Lord Mayor's Procession. I'd better go."

"All right," said Derek. "If you learn more, tell me, and I'll do the same for you."

With a little nod, he hurried away.

"See you later?" asked Alison.

"Meet me at one o'clock, where I store my gear." Robin put his hands on her shoulders, drew her to him, and kissed her.

"I'd like to stay here with you all day," Alison whispered, "but . . ."

Robin hushed her with a finger to her lips. "I know, Her Majesty calls. I should get going, too."

Alison entered the tent in a blissful daze. She made her way to the women's changing room, where the other ladies-in-waiting were getting into costume.

"Hi, Alison," said Tiffany. "How's Robin?"

"He asked for you earlier," Bonnie added. "When we told him you weren't here yet, he was very disappointed."

Alison got her dress. "He's just fine, now. And I'm sure he appreciates your concern."

Sabrina smoothed her skirt over her petticoats. "Can I change the subject? The crowd isn't big today, and Gwen won't like the small turnout. Be careful not to give her an excuse to take out her feelings on us."

"You mean she might not have her usual sunny disposition?" Bonnie asked, with a look of mock alarm.

"Red alert, red alert," called out Maxine.

"Storm warnings will be in effect until further notice."

The only one not taking part in the kidding was Kayla. The prospect of facing Gwen had darkened her mood.

As the procession went through the fairgrounds, Gwen took in the reduced number of customers with a stony expression, and her reaction to the entertainers on the main stage was mechanical and halfhearted. Once offstage, she screamed at a girl who had dropped a banner. But the ladies-in-waiting had done well, and she couldn't find fault with them. As they went to change, Alison saw Derek come into the tent and approach Gwen.

"Has Elissa been here, do you know?"

Gwen let out a bark of mirthless laughter. "Of course not. She's off counting her money and staying out of my sight. Can you believe she didn't fire those leather-sellers who insulted me? Small wonder attendance is down, the way she's botching things."

Alison saw that Kayla had overheard this exchange. While the girls were putting on their street clothes, Kayla nudged her. "Maybe Eric Sinclair isn't the one behind the sabotage. Maybe it's Gwen."

"Gwen wouldn't want MOE destroyed," Alison objected. "She lives to play the queen, and this place provides her only chance. Anyway, I can't see Gwen shooting someone with an arrow, and I'm sure it wasn't Gwen who threatened me last Sunday."

"She's not doing it by herself," answered Kayla. "She'd have accomplices. And she wouldn't want to finish MOE off, just create so much grief for Elissa that she'd finally decide to quit. If Elissa wasn't running the show, maybe Gwen could take over, or at least get her way with whoever replaced Elissa. Then if she wanted someone fired, they'd be gone, period."

Kayla had a point, but Alison still thought Sinclair made a better suspect.

"Gwen could have made the effigy," continued Kayla. "And the day that horse shied, Gwen wasn't using the sedan chair! Maybe she knew the horse would freak out, and didn't want to risk a bad fall. She'd do anything to get control of MOE and be the queen for real."

Alison nodded. "It's a good argument."

"Kayla, Ally!" called Sabrina. "Lunch! Coming?"

As they walked to Oscar's, Alison stopped in her tracks. "Look who's back—again," she whispered to Kayla.

Thirty feet away stood Eric Sinclair, mirrored sunglasses masking his eyes, sipping from a cup. With him was Mr. Tresh, gnawing a beef rib, in jeans and a magenta shirt covered with large red, yellow, and blue circles.

"MOE's most loyal customers," muttered Kayla.

"Look at that shirt," Alison said. "Maybe Mr. Tresh is color-blind."

At that moment, Tresh saw Alison and Kayla,

and said something to Sinclair. Sinclair glanced at them, his eyes unreadable behind his sunglasses. Then the men walked away, toward the main stage. Alison felt edgy. Why did they show up here every day? It certainly wasn't for love of English history.

After lunch Kayla went to see her parents. Alison stayed with the others, waiting for her date with Robin. Time passed too slowly to suit her.

At last it was one o'clock, and she jumped to her feet. "I have to go. See you later."

"Don't be late," warned Sabrina. "Gwen's still ready to blow."

Alison smiled. "This time, I'll be early."

"Tell Robin hello," called Bonnie.

"I always do," Alison replied.

She found Robin going through his props near the fruit-ice stand. "Hi!" he said, smiling, and then turned his attention to the bag. The juggling knives lay on the ground next to him, along with a set of Indian clubs. Looking back in the bag, he groaned.

"I forgot the apples! Hmmm . . . wait a second."

He ducked into the booth and returned carrying some lemons and oranges. "The fruit-ice guys let me borrow these, as long as I return them." He tried juggling three oranges. "These are good. Hey, I could do a fruit juggling routine— apples, oranges, lemons, maybe melons, grapes, bananas. What do you think?"

"I like it," Alison said. "For one thing, you can't burn yourself with an orange."

"Right," Robin said, stowing things in his bag. "It's one of their best features. Let's go!"

They set up in the nearby clearing where he usually performed. Robin blew a blast on the dented bugle, and a decent-sized audience soon gathered. Robin held up three oranges.

"Lords and ladies, this fruit is new to England. It comes from America in the New World," he said, as he began juggling the oranges. "They're called oranges—I can't imagine why. As you can see, they're the ideal juggling fruit. There are rumors that you can eat them, too. I don't know . . . sounds dangerous to me."

The audience grew in number as the act continued. Robin juggled oranges and lemons together, then the Indian clubs, before picking up the lethal-looking knives. Now that Alison realized they posed no real danger, she could relax and enjoy the show.

It took her a moment to sense that something was wrong. Robin's juggling rhythm, normally as precise and regular as a clock, suddenly became ragged. His steady stream of gags stopped. There was a collective gasp from the crowd as the knives fell to the ground, and Robin grabbed his left hand with his right. Blood seeped between his fingers.

With a soft cry, Alison got to her feet and ran to him, taking a handkerchief from her purse. He pressed it against his bleeding hand.

"Thanks," he said. "It's not deep."

"I'm taking you to the infirmary," she said.

"Wait." He raised his voice to carry over the

audience's murmurings. "Don't worry, it's only a scratch! I'll be fine, but this show, unfortunately, is over. Thank you, and enjoy your day in Merrie Olde England."

There was loud applause. As audience members filed away, most put money in Robin's equipment bag.

"Can you pick that up?" Robin began stuffing equipment into the bag. "Something's wrong with those knives, and I have to look them over—"

"*After* the infirmary," insisted Alison.

In the infirmary tent, near the parking lot, an efficient nurse cleaned and dressed the cut. Then Robin and Alison went to a nearby bench, and Robin took out the knives.

He hefted them, and held up one for a closer inspection. Alison leaned in to watch.

"What is it? What happened?"

Robin handed her a knife. "Try balancing it." The handle was unexpectedly heavy, and the knife balanced at the meeting of blade and handle.

"Now this," said Robin, giving her another. The balance point was farther down the blade.

"Why are they different?" Alison asked.

Robin rummaged through his equipment. "I'll show you." Finding a pocket knife, he pried open the handles of the two knives. "Take a look."

Inside one handle were several flat pieces of metal. But the other had a gap where two pieces were missing.

Robin pulled out a weight and handed it to Alison. "Lead weights in the handles make the knives balance correctly. Someone tampered with my stuff."

Alison stared at the knives. "It must have been done between your last two shows today. Anyone messing around in that booth would have been seen."

Robin shook his head. "I didn't use the knives for my first show. In fact, I haven't used them since last Sunday. It could have been done anytime this week."

"They only removed two weights," Alison observed. "Why didn't they take them all?"

"If the difference between the knives had been really big, I'd have felt something wrong before I started. This way, I didn't know till they were in the air." He grinned. "Good thing I don't keep these real sharp. There's not much call for one-handed jugglers."

Alison shuddered. "Don't joke like that! It's not funny—someone really wants to hurt you."

His grin faded. "Yeah, I know. But either I joke about it or I start getting panicky and flip out. I'd rather make jokes."

"Can you work with your hand like that?"

Robin flexed his bandaged hand. "I think so. No knives, for now . . . and no torches. But I'll manage."

Alison looked at her watch and sighed. "I'd better go. I want to be ready for the pageant in plenty of time, for once."

"Meet me in the tent after the show."

Robin drew her to him with his unbandaged

hand, and their lips met in a gentle kiss. There were so many things Alison longed to say, but this wasn't the right time or place.

She kissed him quickly, and said, "Be careful."

"*You* be careful," he said. "They've tried to get me, and they may have something in store for you."

"I know. I'll watch out."

Robin hesitated, like he wanted to say more.

"What is it?" she asked.

He released her. "It'll keep. You have to go."

For once, Alison could take her time getting ready for the Queen's Pageant. As she did, she told a shocked Kayla what had happened to Robin.

"Was it a bad cut?"

"No. Luckily the knives aren't very sharp. But we're making someone nervous."

Kayla bit her lip. "You sure are—me! I'm scared that you're getting in too deep."

Alison shrugged. "I'll be all right."

In addition to the crowd, four TV cameras showed up for the Queen's Pageant. Gwen was on her best behavior. The crafts were shown, and then a rope was strung several feet above the stage, under Billy's supervision. After a fanfare, Zach announced, "Your Majesty, Ladies and Gentlemen . . . The Great Alfredo!"

A short, wiry man swung himself onto the rope and began a graceful acrobatic act. Alison was impressed—he moved as easily on the rope as she did on a sidewalk. As his stunts grew more difficult, the applause became longer and louder.

He was standing on one foot, balancing long poles on both hands, when the rope parted. Alfredo fell to the plywood with a thud, the poles clattering around him.

Afterward, Alison couldn't remember if one of the screams she heard was her own.

CHAPTER 9

Zach rushed forward from his place near the throne and knelt beside the stunned acrobat.

"Don't try to move," he said, his voice calm and low. "We'll get medical attention for you right away." Alison saw the man speak, but couldn't hear what he said. Zach bent closer to hear him.

Billy spoke urgently into his walkie-talkie. Gwen remained on the throne, silent and immobile.

"How is he?" called a voice from the audience.

Zach beckoned to Derek, at the rear of the stage. After a hurried conference, Zach turned to the audience. "Attention, please. We won't be sure of Alfredo's condition until a doctor sees him, but he's conscious and talking. Experienced acrobats know how to minimize injury when they fall. He says he doubts any bones are broken. As soon as we can, we'll pass the word on how he's doing. Now, let's give Alfredo the Great the ovation he deserves."

There was thunderous applause.

The audience dispersed. In place of the usual stately exit, people simply walked off the stage, talking quietly among themselves.

Alison looked around. Billy was watching Alfredo being put on a stretcher. The rope lay where it had fallen. She knelt down to give it a careful look.

The rope was half an inch in diameter. Part of the end was frayed and tangled, as if it had given way strand by strand. But part of it . . . Alison stared at the end intently. Part of the rope wasn't frayed at all. The strands were separated in one place—as if the rope had been cut or sawed partway through, then allowed to break under Alfredo's weight.

The fall had been caused by cold-blooded sabotage.

Alfredo might have been badly hurt, or even killed! Who could she tell about her discovery? Robin wasn't around. Maybe Derek . . .

"Hey! What do you think you're doing?"

Billy Hawley snatched the rope from her hands.

"Looking for a souvenir? Beat it! You've got no business here, and you're in the way!"

"But it wasn't an accident!" Alison protested. "Look at the rope! It was cut partway—"

Billy's smile was mocking. "Oh, yeah? Listen to the ace detective! And all this time I thought you were just a dumb kid with a big imagination!"

"Just look at the way the—"

Billy crowded her backward, forcing Alison to retreat. "Listen, Nancy Drew, get out of my face and leave this to people who know what they're doing! Now!"

Alison had no choice but to leave Billy in possession of the rope.

Going backstage, she found a storm raging. Gwen was at the center of it, screaming at Derek.

"How could such a dreadful thing be allowed to happen? I want an explanation!"

Kayla, already in her street clothes, nudged Alison's arm and rolled her eyes. "She's at it again."

"She's upset about poor Alfredo," Alison whispered back. "So is everyone else. It was dreadful."

"That's not it," said Kayla. "As far as she's concerned, the worst thing that happened out there is that she was made to look bad—on TV, too."

Alison couldn't believe even Gwen was that self-centered. But Kayla was right.

"What stupidity, to have an acrobat perform in my pageant!" Gwen snapped, glaring at Derek. "A careless acrobat with shabby equipment turns the fair's finest event into a bad piece of slapstick comedy!"

"Gwen!" Elissa had arrived in time to hear the last part of Gwen's tirade. She looked older and very tired . . . and furious.

"Gwen, be in my office in ten minutes." She raised her voice. "Happily, Alfredo suffered only

scrapes and bruises. He'll be fine in a day or two."
She hurried out, looking frazzled, followed by
Derek.

As she left, a gloating smile appeared under
Gwen's heavy makeup. Why was she so pleased?

Elissa and Derek left before Alison had a
chance to tell them about the rope. Then Kayla
raced by. "Have to run! I'm filling in for Kaye for
awhile. Let's get burritos later."

Kayla almost collided with Robin at the tent
entrance. "Still in costume?" he asked, coming up
to Alison.

"Give me two minutes," she replied. "Did you
hear about the accident during the pageant?"

"The acrobat? Yeah, someone told me."

"After I change I'll tell you what I found."

A few minutes later, she led Robin to a quiet
corner of the tent and told him about the rope.

When she'd finished he asked, "Who else
have you told about this?"

"No one. I tried to tell Billy, but he wouldn't
listen. In fact, he ordered me off the stage."

"Where's the rope now?" Robin asked.

Alison shrugged. "Maybe it's still out front."

"Come on, let's take a look."

But when they got to the front of the stage, the
rope was gone. The stage was empty, except for
Wolfgang and another musician putting away their
instruments.

"Yo, Wolfgang!" Robin called.

Wolfgang trudged to the front of the stage.

"Rough day?" Robin asked him.

The musician sat on his trumpet case. "This isn't a fun gig. There must be a hex on poor old MOE. That guy falls . . . I don't know . . . it's a bad scene."

"About that fall—" Alison started to say.

Robin instantly cut her off.

"Did you see if Billy took the rope when he left?"

"I wasn't looking. My main interest in Billy is staying out of his way. But he must've taken it. It was there, and now it's gone, and so is he." Wolfgang stood up. "I've got to rehearse for tonight. What are you doing—" He noticed Robin's bandaged hand. "Hey, what happened to you?"

"A little accident, no big deal. I'm okay."

Wolfgang sighed. "You see? This place is hexed. Later."

As he walked away, Alison turned to Robin. "Why did you interrupt me?"

"I don't think we should talk about what's going on here, except to Elissa, Derek, and Kayla."

"Don't tell me you suspect Wolfgang!"

"No," he answered. "But if we tell people, even friends, they'll tell their friends. Soon everyone will know what we're up to, and that someone's pulling dirty, dangerous tricks. It could start a panic, and then we'd be more of a target than we already are."

"I guess," Alison said.

Robin looked at his watch. "I want to try using different kinds of fruit in the red lantern show tonight, like I talked about earlier. Let's see what I can get at the ice booth."

As they walked along, holding hands, Alison thought about herself and Robin. Being with him felt good and natural, as if she'd known him forever. But they had only met ten days before. Was she making a big mistake? Was it foolish to feel so drawn to a boy she'd known for such a short time? There was a lot she didn't know about him. Did he have other girlfriends? Maybe one special girlfriend who was away for the summer? Alison might be just a summertime fling for him.

She desperately wanted an answer to one big question: How deep were his feelings for her?

In her last school year in Connecticut she'd really liked a boy named Devlin. Handsome and funny, he flirted with her for weeks before they went out together. After their second date, she was certain that she and Devlin were meant for each other.

But their second date turned out to be their last. Devlin had dumped her for someone else, without hesitation or explanation. Alison had ached for a long time afterward. She never wanted that to happen again.

Alison realized that he was watching her as they walked. "What are you thinking about?" he asked.

She squeezed his hand. "Oh, nothing special." Only my future happiness, she thought.

Sid, the man who sold the fruit ices, told Robin to help himself from the bin in back of the booth. Robin chose oranges, lemons, peaches, and limes. As he worked, he explained that the ices tasted so good because there was pureed fresh fruit in each batch.

He started to peel an orange. Alison was mystified. "They'll be messy to juggle when they're peeled," she said.

"I'm only doing this to one," Robin told her. "You know how I eat an apple while I juggle it? I want to try that with an orange in the show tonight. It's a crowd-pleaser. Also," he said, grinning, "I'm hungry."

Robin took the peel to a trash barrel. As he deposited it, he did a double take. "What's this doing here?"

He reached in and came up with a slender, shiny object. It was a clear, plastic, hypodermic syringe, with an inch-long needle.

"That's a weird place for a syringe," Alison said.

"Maybe someone with diabetes used it and threw it there," suggested Robin.

Alison shook her head. "I don't think so. I have a friend back in Connecticut who gives himself insulin injections. The syringes and needles are smaller. Also, you shouldn't dump these anywhere—a little kid might find it."

Robin took Alison's handkerchief out of his pouch, and wrapped the syringe in it. "We'll drop this at the infirmary later." He put it into his equipment bag.

"Now, let's see if this works," Robin said, taking the peeled orange and two unpeeled ones, and tossing them in the air. "It's not too messy—

yet. Maybe after it's been bitten, it will be. Here goes—"

"Robin, no!" Alison leaped forward and knocked Robin's hand away from his mouth before he could take a bite. The orange hit the dusty ground with a squish.

"Hey, that's my bad hand!" Robin shook it and winced.

"Sorry, it's just . . . I had an idea. Maybe it's totally crazy, but I didn't want to take a chance, because if I'm right—"

"Alison, slow down!" Robin exclaimed.

"Sorry. I asked myself, what's a hypodermic doing here, especially a humongous one like that? And I thought, they make ices here with fresh fruit, which they keep in that bin, which anyone could open. See?"

Robin stared at her, openmouthed. "No, I don't see."

"Last weekend it was the lemonade. They wouldn't poison the lemonade again, because everyone's watching that stuff like hawks. But what about the ices? They could put something into the ices—"

Robin's eyes widened. "By injecting poison into the fruit!" he finished. "Oh, wow! Come on, we have to tell Sid!"

They raced to the front of the booth. "Did you find what you need back there?" Sid asked.

"This sounds crazy," Robin said, "but we think your ices may be poisoned!"

Sid looked up from arranging containers in his

freezer. "Robin, don't joke about things like that. Not after last weekend."

"It's no joke," insisted Robin. He put the handkerchief on the counter, and displayed the syringe. "We found this in the trash next to your booth."

As Alison explained her hunch, Sid turned pale. "This is awful," he groaned. "Let's check it out."

He fastened a wooden shutter over the counter, and went around back with Robin and Alison. "Let's see if we can find anything," he said.

"Was that syringe at the bottom of the trash or the top?" Alison asked.

"Near the top," replied Robin. "I see what you're getting at—it hasn't been there long. If something was injected into the fruit, it was done recently."

Sid was examining oranges from a bag. "Today has been slow, so we haven't sold all of what we made this morning. But I just put a new batch in the freezer."

"Let's see what we find here," said Alison, as she and Robin took some oranges out of the bag.

A minute later Robin said, "Look at this."

Alison peered at the orange in his hand. There was a tiny but unmistakable puncture in the skin.

"Here's another," exclaimed Sid, showing the others. "I'd never have noticed a needle mark like this if I hadn't been looking for it. I'll dump what we made this afternoon, and all this fruit, too."

"Not yet," cautioned Alison. "Keep it for testing—and for evidence, once we find out who did it."

Sid nodded. "I'll mark it all, so no one uses it by

mistake. You two saved me a lot of grief. Thanks."

"Alison figured it out," Robin said. "Thank her."

Sid smiled. "Normally, I'd offer you as many ices as you could eat, on the house, but . . ."

"I'll take a rain check," said Alison.

"They didn't inject all the oranges," Robin said.

"Last week, they didn't poison all the lemonade concentrate," observed Alison. "I guess it's enough if just a few people get sick."

"What now?" Sid wanted to know.

Robin said, "Alison and I will take some of this stuff to Elissa and tell her what we found. We won't discuss this with anyone else."

As they gathered the evidence together, Alison asked, "Sid, did you notice anybody hanging around this afternoon?"

Sid thought a moment. "There were customers, vendors, performers, security guys. I wasn't paying much attention . . . wait a second, there was one guy. He bought ices and I saw him looking around a little later. And when I went to dump something in the trash, he was hanging around in back of the booth. Before I could ask what he wanted, he walked away. I probably wouldn't have noticed it was the same guy, but I don't think there are two shirts like that in the world."

Alison felt as if she'd been given a jolt of electricity. "His shirt? What about it?"

"It was a nightmare, big red, yellow, and blue polka dots on a purple background."

There was no possible doubt. The man hanging around by the booth had been Mr. Tresh.

10

"You've seen that shirt, huh?" Robin asked as they headed for Elissa's office with bags of fruit and the syringe.

"Uh-huh," she replied. "On Mr. Tresh."

"Always in the wrong place at the right time!"

As they approached the office a woman came out, wearing a flower-print dress, her dark hair in a bun. Alison was startled to see Gwen out of Queen Elizabeth regalia. In ordinary clothes, she looked so . . . ordinary.

"Her Maj looks upset," Robin said.

"I wonder why," remarked Alison.

"Another fight with Elissa," Robin guessed as he knocked on the office door.

"Come in," called Elissa.

The office was small, with Merrie Olde England posters from past years on the pine-paneled walls. Elissa sat at her desk with Derek across from her.

Elissa leaned back and closed her eyes. "Is this important? If not . . ."

"It's very important." Alison said, as she and Robin put their bags on Elissa's desk.

"What's this?" asked Derek, looking into a bag. "Oranges!" He pulled one out. "Yum!"

"Put that back!" shouted Robin.

Elissa sat up straight. "What's going on?"

Robin explained about the syringe in the trash barrel.

"This fruit," Alison went on, "has been injected with something, probably some kind of poison."

Derek dropped the orange as if it were red-hot. Alison said, "Eric Sinclair's friend Tresh was seen by the booth around the time this happened."

"This is like a bad dream." Elissa's voice was faint. "Has anyone gotten sick?"

"We're lucky," Robin replied. "The ices from this morning were all right, and they hadn't started selling the new batch yet, because business was slow today."

"Thank goodness the TV people are gone. It's bad enough they saw Alfredo's accident. If they'd heard about this—"

"About Alfredo," Alison said. "I don't think it was an accident."

She described what the rope had looked like, and her guess as to what caused the fall.

"How could it be?" Derek asked. "If someone did that in front of that crowd, it would have been seen."

"I'm just telling you what I saw," said Alison.

"I don't have a clue how it was done."

"Sinclair and Tresh are up to something. Can't you stop them?" demanded Derek. "Bring in the police, maybe."

Elissa rubbed her eyes wearily. "We have no evidence. Nobody saw Tresh poison oranges, or shoot an arrow, or cut a rope. Unless he left fingerprints on the syringe, which I doubt, the police can't act. And if we call them, the press will get wind of it. We'd get headlines like SIEGE OF TERROR AT THE FAIR! We wouldn't be able to give tickets away."

"There must be a way to beat them," said Derek.

"If anyone has a plan, I'd love to hear it," said Elissa. "Meanwhile, I'll tell Billy to have Sinclair and Tresh watched. Maybe we'll catch them in the act."

"This may sound crazy," Alison said, "but could Gwen be involved in this?"

Derek snorted. "Ridiculous!"

"She doesn't like the way you run things. Maybe she wants someone else to take over. Maybe she'd like to do it herself," Alison went on.

Elissa smiled. "Gwen couldn't run a tea party. This fair is a big business."

"Indeed it is," said Derek.

"Gwen looked steamed just now, leaving the office. Did you have a fight?" Robin asked.

Elissa glared with remembered anger. "I was furious with her for her selfish attitude about Alfredo. She acted as though the only thing that mattered was that she'd been made to look bad. Then she accused me of caring more about ticket sales than the spirit of Merrie Olde England. She said it'll be my fault if we fail. She *could* be involved, but, like Derek, I find it hard to believe."

"What should we do now?" Alison asked.

"I'll speak to Billy," Derek offered. "I'll have him keep security on their toes, and have Sinclair and his henchman watched at all times."

Elissa smiled. "Thanks. It's getting to be too much for me, I'm afraid. Let's try to keep this quiet. Alison, Robin—I don't know how to thank you. Please, be careful. Let's not have anyone else hurt."

As they left the office, Alison realized she was starving. "I'm meeting Kayla for burritos," she said. "Come with us."

Robin shook his head. He looked troubled, his expression distant. "I have to rehearse for tonight," he said. He paused, then seemed to come to a decision. "Look, meet me by the tent after my act, okay? We'll find a place to talk."

Alison's heart lurched. Why did he look so serious? What did he want to tell her? Was it something she wouldn't want to hear?

Alison forced herself to smile and say, "Sure."

"See you then, I guess," Robin said. He walked away without a smile, without a kiss. A terrible certainty chilled her soul.

He doesn't want to see me. Alison felt as if she'd turned to stone. It was just like what happened with Devlin, except this would hurt a lot more.

Her father liked to say, "If something looks too good to be true, it probably is."

Father does know best.

She and Kayla went for burritos. Somehow, she ate half of hers, though it was like eating ashes. As Kayla chatted, Alison gave mechanical answers. It didn't feel right to dump her problems in Kayla's lap.

She was so lost in gloom that she didn't realize Kayla had stopped talking and was staring at her. "Alison? Are you okay? You look like you just got some bad news."

Alison tried to smile, but tears trickled down her cheeks. "S-sorry," she murmured, even unhappier at the idea of being a public spectacle.

She fumbled for a handkerchief, then remembered she'd given it to Robin. Kayla handed her a tissue.

"What's wrong?" Kayla clasped Alison's hands.

"It—it's Robin," Alison finally said. "I really like him, but . . . he doesn't feel that way about me."

"What? Robin's crazy about you," protested Kayla.

"I think he did like me, but now he doesn't. Maybe I scared him off. I've never had a real boyfriend, ever. This time, I'd hoped . . . oh, never mind, it doesn't matter."

"It can't be," said Kayla. "When Robin's not with you, he's checking with us, asking where you are. The girls joke about it, and they all know what's happening. Majority rules—we're right, and you're wrong."

Alison sighed. "I don't think so, but thanks for making me feel a little better."

"You're welcome. Now here's my plan. We let Kaye and Larry buy us churros, we get seats for the show, we have a great time. All in favor, raise their hands."

Alison had to laugh as she stuck her hand in the air. "It's a very excellent plan. Let's do it."

At seven-thirty, Alison sat with the Martínezes in front of the main stage, along with hundreds of other fair workers, family members, and friends. The stage was lit by portable spotlights, and the evening was balmy.

Wolfgang and his musicians appeared and bowed, to applause and whistles. Zach entered in jeans, a silk top hat, and a T-shirt that read HIZZONER.

"Ladies and gents," he intoned, "it's show time." There were whoops and hollers. "For those who haven't seen a red lantern show, any resemblance between it and MOE is purely accidental. So, kick back, relax, forget those 'thees' and 'thous', and let's party!"

The audience howled. Zach held up a hand.

"We'll kick things off with some music. Let's put our hands together for Wolfgang's Wonderful Wind Works!"

The band played pop tunes arranged like old English dance music, and old English tunes arranged like rock. Wolfgang finished with a bluesy, vocal rendition of "Greensleeves." The crowd shouted its approval.

"Next," said Zach, "we have the most talented, funniest, most popular act in the history of Merrie Olde England. If you don't believe it, just ask him. Here he is, a legend in his own mind . . . Robin Goodfellow!"

Alison cheered, too, but her painful emotions returned as she watched him. Robin juggled apples, oranges, lemons, limes, bananas, even cantaloupes. He had five pieces of fruit going at once when Wolfgang ran on in a hideous dress, a red fright wig, and a cardboard crown, a Styrofoam sword in hand.

"Off with his head!" he shrieked in a piercing falsetto. "He's disrespectful to my Royal Highness!"

Robin dropped his fruit and tore around the stage, while Wolfgang chased him, swinging the sword. The audience ate it up. Suddenly, Wolfgang turned to face the hooting, whistling crowd. "Long live me!" he bellowed. "Bow to me, you scurvy knaves! Right now!"

A babble of shouted insults was the response. Wolfgang yelled, "I'm the queen! If you don't bow, I'll . . . I'll hold my breath till I turn blue!"

Robin tiptoed forward with a pie plate full of whipped cream and shoved it into Wolfgang's face. The audience erupted into cheers and laughter.

Alison turned to Kayla. "Does Gwen come to these shows?"

"Her Maj? Are you kidding? It's beneath her."

Once Wolfgang ran off, Robin finished his act, and left the stage to enthusiastic applause. Alison felt her nerves tighten, and nudged Kayla. "See you later."

Kayla gave her a hug. "Okay. My fingers are crossed."

Alison went around the stage to the tent. She stood in the dimness, hearing laughter from the crowd. A couple exited the tent and smiled at Alison. The boy put an arm around the girl as they passed her.

Waiting, Alison began to feel calmer. It's not Robin's fault he feels the way he does, she thought.

Robin emerged from the tent a few minutes later. "Sorry I took so long. I locked up my stuff where nobody can mess with it."

"It's okay," Alison replied, surprised at how cool she felt. "You were great. How's the hand?"

He flexed it and shrugged. "I can work with it. Um . . . where can we go to talk?"

"How about up the hill?" Alison gestured to where the processions formed. "It'll be quiet and private."

As they climbed, Robin didn't take her hand, and Alison felt a chasm opening between them. A half moon came from behind a cloud, dimly lighting their way.

"There are lots of rumors backstage," he said. "Word is getting around about poisoned drinks and snipers with bows and arrows. There's real fear in the air."

Fear . . . Alison turned to Robin, shedding her anxieties for the moment. "I almost forgot. The first day I was here, I had this bizarre dream."

She told him about it as they reached the top of the hill. She told him what the dream voices had said: *We have to put fear into her. Even if people get hurt . . . or worse.* "It seemed so real, I thought maybe it wasn't a dream at all. Now, I wonder if I didn't actually overhear this thing being planned."

"Were the voices familiar?" asked Robin.

Alison thought hard, but finally shook her head. "I remember the words, but not the voices."

"Were they men's voices?"

"I can't even remember that. It's so frustrating!" She looked at the fair spread out below. Robin stood alongside her, and for a moment, neither spoke. Finally, Robin broke the silence.

"I have to talk to you, but . . . it's tough. I don't know how to start, or anything."

"I know." Alison didn't look at him. "Some things are hard to say."

"I guess." He plucked a dandelion and twirled it between his fingers. "It's funny, my friends all have girlfriends, but I never did."

Alison was surprised; Robin was cute enough to attract plenty of girls. "How come?" she asked.

"Between school, and work, and practicing my juggling, I'm always busy. Getting involved with a girl always seemed like a distraction. When I think one is getting serious, I back off. So now . . ." He stopped, looking very ill at ease.

Alison realized that she could make this easier for them both by giving Robin the impression that she wasn't looking for romance, either. She was sure the prospect of hurting her was making him feel bad.

"I sometimes give guys the wrong idea of how I feel about them," Alison said. "I mean, sometimes one will think I . . . really like him, but—"

"—but you aren't serious about him at all," finished Robin. "Is that it?"

"That's it," she said. I have to do this, she thought. Why should we both feel awful?

"Oh," he said. "I figured you might want—"

"I like you," she said quickly. "Really. I enjoy being with you. But you shouldn't feel that I'm . . . looking for something more."

"Uh-huh. Okay." Robin smiled, and Alison felt relieved. She'd done the right thing. "I get the message. It's good we talked. Want to go back down now?"

"Sure," Alison replied. "Unless there was something more you wanted to say."

"Me? Nope. We both understand how we feel, and that's the important thing. Come on, we can catch the last part of the show."

As they started down, Alison fought off an urge to blurt out the truth about her feelings. What would be the point?

As they walked the moon vanished behind another cloud, leaving them in almost pitch-blackness. Alison stumbled and nearly tripped over a rock.

"What happened?" called Robin. "Are you okay?"

"I'm all right," she called back. "It's hard to

see where I'm going without moonlight."

In front and to the left of her, she made out towering silhouettes of trees, and knew they were skirting the upper edge of the grove—"their" grove, she'd called it. It wasn't theirs now. Nothing was.

Robin was between her and the trees. "Take it slow," he called out. "There are some tricky—oof!"

He crashed to the ground. At the same instant, Alison heard something zip close by her and thud into a tree. She hurried forward.

"Robin? Where are you? Are you hurt?"

She almost stepped on him, sprawled on the ground. A huge oak tree loomed up in her path. Deeply embedded in its trunk was an arrow.

Someone had shot at them!

CHAPTER 1

Alison tried not to panic. Someone was out there, in the dark, armed and ready to kill! She felt exposed and defenseless. There might be an arrow aimed at them right now! She knelt down next to Robin.

"Robin?" she whispered. "Are you hurt?"

"I'm okay," he muttered. "Just skinned my knee. I lost my footing when I—"

"Somebody shot an arrow at us!"

He froze. "What?"

"It's in the tree over your head. It might have hit you if you hadn't fallen."

Something that sounded like a giant insect buzzed by Alison's ear, frighteningly close. "Another one! Who—"

"Get behind the tree!" he snapped. "Stay low!"

As they scrambled for cover, another arrow whizzed by, into the grove behind them.

They huddled there waiting for the attacker's

next move. Nothing happened.

Alison peered in the direction the arrows had come from. She heard Robin moving next to her. A dark silhouette moved against a slightly lighter background.

She heard a footstep. Someone was on the hillside, thirty feet away and coming closer. She tapped Robin on the shoulder.

"I know," he said. "I'm going to try something."

He stepped into the open, his arm cocked, and something in his hand. He threw it hard, and ducked behind the tree.

There was a thunk and the shadowy figure grunted.

Alison whispered, "What did you—"

"I threw a rock. I wanted to make the guy think twice about coming after us."

Alison looked up. The moon silvered the edge of a cloud. "The moon's coming out!"

The stalker also must have realized that he'd soon be visible to his intended victims. Footsteps hastily moved away. The mystery assailant was taking off.

Robin jumped up and ran after the retreating archer. Alison moved, too, but more slowly, uneasy about running full speed over rough terrain in dim light. She saw something on the ground where the attacker had been and bent to get it. It was a bow. A few arrows lay scattered nearby.

She could hear running footsteps across the slope, near the beginning of another wooded area. She stayed in place, anxious, wishing Robin hadn't been so impulsive. Maybe the person was still armed. Then she saw Robin walking toward her.

"I lost him in those trees," he said, breathing hard. "But I know who it was."

"You do? How?"

"Just before the guy made it to the trees, I got a look at his shirt. It was covered with big circles."

Alison gasped. "Tresh!"

"Exactly." Robin flashed a triumphant smile. "And we caught him in the act. Let's find Elissa and give her the good news. Now, she can bring in the police and end this once and for all."

Alison felt like hugging Robin, but stopped herself. It wouldn't be right, after their little talk on the hill. It would make them both uncomfortable.

They found Elissa watching the show from the back of the audience. She heard their story, and her eyes flashed with anger.

"I'm calling the police right now. My guess is, once Mr. Tresh is in custody, he'll testify against Sinclair to get a lighter sentence." She started to go, but turned back. "If you see Derek or Billy, tell them what you told me, and have them meet me in the office. Oh, and the police will want to hear your story as well. Can you stick around and see them?"

"I'll stay," offered Robin. "I don't think Alison has anything to add to what I say, and she needs a ride home from Larry and Kaye Martínez. They'll probably want to leave as soon as the show ends."

"That's reasonable," Elissa said. "Go ahead and get your ride, Alison. You've done enough for today."

"Okay. Good night." As Elissa left for the office, Alison found herself face to face with Robin.

"Well," she said, "I guess I'll find Kayla and her folks. You sure I don't have to wait for the police?"

"I don't see why. If they need to, they can talk to you tomorrow or call you at home. I'll give them your phone number."

"Okay, then." Alison felt very awkward, and Robin appeared to feel the same way. Neither one knew how to end this strained conversation.

"I'll see you tomorrow," she said finally. "My parents and sister are coming, and I want them to see your show. Maybe you can cheer Dana up."

Robin's grin was dry. "I'll do my best. Well . . . take it easy."

Alison watched him walk away, wishing at that moment that she'd never heard of MOE. It was true that MOE had saved her from a boring summer and the painful adjustment period the rest of her family was going through. But now she knew there were worse things in life than boredom.

On Sunday morning the waiting crowd was still small. But the Martínezes were sure things would be back to normal the following weekend. The night before Alison had told Kayla and her parents that Tresh and Sinclair were probably under arrest by now, and the fair's troubles were over.

Mr. Martínez parked the van. He and his wife unloaded it, while Alison and Kayla walked toward the performers' tent. Neither Martínez parent bothered to warn Kayla about poisoned drinks or food. The crisis was over.

At the entrance to the fairgrounds, Derek trotted up, in costume. He swept off his hat and bowed deeply.

"Good morrow, ladies! 'Tis an occasion for great cheer, is it not? And Lady Alison has proven herself a splendid detective!"

"Hi, Derek," said Alison. "What's new? Are Sinclair and Tresh behind bars?"

"Not yet." Derek switched to modern English. "The police haven't found them. There's no sign of Sinclair at his office or home. His wife doesn't know where he is. As for Mr. Tresh, not only don't the police know where he is, they don't even know *who* he is."

"What are you talking about?" demanded Kayla.

"The police haven't located anyone named Tresh in Southern California who could be the man with Sinclair. Either he comes from someplace else, or he's using an alias. Either way, it looks suspicious, doesn't it?"

Alison frowned. "Then they're still around."

"Don't worry," Derek assured her. "They'll turn up. And they'd be crazy to come here." He lowered his voice. "Merrie Olde England is crawling with plainclothes police today." He winked.

"That's good to know," said Alison, anxious to escape. "We'd better go. See you."

She and Kayla had no sooner walked away

when Robin practically bumped into them. He tried to look cool and casual, but Alison sensed his discomfort.

"Hi," she said. "How's the hand?"

"Almost back to normal. Is your family here?"

"Not yet. They're meeting me after the Lord Mayor's Procession."

"Your sister, too?"

"You mean Little Miss Sunshine? Yes, her, too, wrapped in her cloud of gloom and doom."

"Bring them to my show. I bet I make her laugh."

"You're a great juggler, but to make Dana laugh, you'd have to be a magician. Well, we'd better get into costume."

As the girls walked away, Kayla stole a glance over her shoulder. "He's still watching you. Alison, are you absolutely sure you're right about Robin?"

"Absolutely, positively, one hundred percent. Look, Kayla, I really don't want to talk about him."

They walked the rest of the way in silence.

12

The ladies-in-waiting climbed the hill for the procession. As they reached the top, Kayla pointed. "Hey, the horses are back!"

"Elissa must think it's safe, with Sinclair and Tresh on the run," Alison said.

Alison was looking forward to taking her family around the fair and introducing them to her friends. They had been in a good mood that morning, apparently eager for a change of scene.

Alison spotted them by Oscar's barbecue booth while the procession went through the grounds. Mrs. Crisp waved excitedly, and pointed her out to Dana and Mr. Crisp, who shouldered his camcorder. Alison thought she saw a trace of a smile on Dana's face.

"Ally!" Mrs. Crisp called. "Over here! Hi, honey!" Her father waved with one hand while aiming the camcorder with the other. Alison laughed and waved back, glad to see them all happy. She kept waving, turning back toward them as the procession passed.

"Pssst! Alison!" Kayla pointed to Gwen, glaring down from her sedan chair. Quickly, Alison faced front, face set in the official, ladies-in-waiting smile. She knew Gwen would have something to say to her later.

Luckily, Gwen left to pose for pictures after the procession, so Alison was spared a scene with her. She threw on her regular clothes and ran to meet the Crisps by the stage, hugging each of them in turn.

"You looked lovely!" exclaimed her mother.

"You sure did—and I've got it on videotape!" announced her father.

"It was okay," Dana said, hugging Alison back.

Alison kept an arm around Dana. "I'm glad you came! The other girls are at Oscar's, having lunch."

"Lunch? Sounds great," said Mr. Crisp.

"Alison! What'll it be?" boomed Oscar, when they got to his booth.

"Oscar, meet my mom, my dad, and my sister, Dana. Oscar makes Old English barbecue—"

"—which is a lot like regular barbecue," Oscar said. "Alison's a great girl. Chicken or beef ribs?"

As they took their food, Kayla called from under a nearby tree. "Come on over! We've saved you room!"

Wolfgang, who was sitting with the girls, flashed a grin. "What ho, Lady Alison! Is this your family?" He jumped up. "Hi, Mr. Crisp. Mrs. Crisp, a pleasure." He bowed, and looked quizzically at Dana. "And this is . . . don't tell me, I'll guess. Let's see, you're not her mom or dad . . . you're not an elderly grandparent . . . you must be . . . uhhh . . . ummmm . . ."

Dana grinned broadly. "I'm Ally's sister."

Wolfgang snapped his fingers. "That was my next guess! Wolfgang's the name, music's my game. Alison's a great human being, beautiful, smart—she'd get my vote for queen if we didn't already have one. Gotta run, a musician's work is never done. Bye!"

And he was off, leaving the Crisps staring after him.

Dana said, "He's funny, in a weird way."

The family greeted Kayla and met the others, and sat down to eat. "Where's Queen Elizabeth?" asked Mrs. Crisp. "Will we meet her, too?"

"I don't think so," said Alison.

"She's . . . pretty busy," Kayla added.

"She certainly looks the part," Mr. Crisp remarked. "Very royal, if you know what I mean."

"Oh, we know, all right," said Bonnie.

After they'd finished, Alison said, "While I have time, let me show you around."

She took them on a tour, ending at Kayla Krafts. Mrs. Crisp bought a handbag, Mr. Crisp got a hand-tooled belt, and Dana chose a leather brooch.

"What next?" asked Mr. Crisp.

They heard the ugly blast of a badly played bugle.

Dana made a face. "What's that noise?"

"It's someone I want you to see," said Alison.

They found Robin arranging his gear. He saw Alison, nodded, and went back to his equipment.

Dana nudged Alison. "You know him? He's cute!"

"Yes, I know him."

Robin picked up three rubber balls. "Lords and ladies, good day! Robin Goodfellow, at your service." He quickly had the balls flying, his hands virtually motionless. His eyes went through the crowd and came to rest on Dana. "I know what you're thinking: 'Eeew, a juggler! Gross!'"

Dana smiled.

"I'm going to tell you the history of juggling. It was invented by Harvey Muttonfat, a cook for King Henry the Eighth. Henry's favorite food was baked turnips—potatoes weren't invented yet." Down went the clubs. He scooped up a handful of white turnips.

"One day the King ordered baked turnips, straight from the oven. 'But, Sire,' said Harvey, 'there isn't a clean dish in the palace, and the turnips are too hot to handle.' 'If they aren't out here in one minute, you're dead meat!' yelled the King.

"So Harvey opened the oven and picked up the turnips. 'Ooooh-ooow,' he screamed. 'These things are hot!'" Robin tossed up the turnips he was holding and began juggling them. "He didn't want to be dead meat, so he carried them into the dining room that way."

"Henry was amazed. 'Amazing!' he said. 'What do you call that, anyway?' 'I call it juggling, Sire,' said Harvey. 'Why?' asked the King. 'I don't know, Sire, it looks like juggling to me.' And that's how juggling began. The next important event in the history of juggling is me. Thank you very much." He caught the turnips, and bowed.

There was laughter and applause. Dana laughed along with everyone else. Robin did ten more minutes, finishing with the flaming torches, which earned him a standing ovation.

The audience drifted off, and Robin started putting his props away. Alison came up him.

"You were fantastic. And you made Dana laugh."

He shrugged. "That's my strong suit, making a good first impression."

"They'd like to meet you, if that's okay."

"Sure," he said. "I'd like that."

She made the introductions. Robin was pleasant and thanked them for their compliments. Mr. and Mrs. Crisp were charmed, while Dana was totally awed.

"I have to get ready for the Queen's Pageant," said Alison. "Will you stay for that?"

""We wouldn't miss it," said her father. "You go get ready, and we'll meet you by the stage at—" He checked his watch "—at four o'clock."

Alison smiled. "Great!" She turned to Robin, who had packed his equipment. "See you."

"Uh-huh. Nice meeting you all." He picked up his bag and walked away.

"Those dimples are adorable!" Dana said.

"He's really something," said Mr. Crisp.

Mrs. Crisp nodded. "Very talented. Don't you think so, Ally?"

"Yes. Well, see you later."

In the changing room, Sabrina called, "Listen, everyone: Gwen heard that Wolfgang made fun of her at the red lantern show last night, and she's really hot. Watch out."

"It was just a joke!" exclaimed Alison. "Doesn't she have a sense of humor?"

Sabrina shook her head. "In four years I've never seen a sign of one. Be ready for an explosion."

The pageant went well and there was no hint of a coming explosion from Gwen. Alison even risked waving to her family again.

As she entered the tent, she grinned at Sabrina. "Guess she cooled off, huh?"

A voice rang out behind her. "Stop right there, you rude little brat! I want a word with you!"

Alison spun around to find Gwen heading for her, quivering with rage. "What do you mean, dropping character and flapping your arms in front of thousands of people! I was mortified! How dare you!"

Alison felt her own anger building. "How dare I wave to my family? You've got to be kidding!"

"Don't get snippy! While you're in my court, you have no family! Your only concern is the queen! The real Queen Elizabeth would have had you whipped for lack of respect!"

"Maybe so, if she was as nasty as you!" Alison was too steamed up to stop. "But you're not the queen and I'm not your servant! So get out of my face!"

Gwen's eyes bulged and her jaw dropped. "I should slap your face for that!"

"Don't touch her!" Robin shoved through the onlookers and strode into the tent, staring defiantly at Gwen "It's about time someone told you where to get off!"

"I'll make an example of you both," Gwen hissed. "From now on people will know their place around here! I'm going to find Elissa and—"

"I'm right here, Gwen." Elissa emerged from the changing room in street clothes.

"You heard them abuse and insult me?" Gwen asked.

"I heard," said Elissa, looking sad. "I've been inattentive to what's been going on around here. I should have acted a long time ago."

"Yes," said Gwen. "But better late than never."

"True," Elissa agreed. "I'm sorry, Gwen, but I'm going to have to replace you."

Gwen blinked. "Replace . . . me? But . . . you can't!"

"Of course I can," said Elissa. "I hired you and I can fire you. Any actress who fits the wardrobe can play the queen. There are no lines to learn. She just has to sit on a throne and smile."

Gwen's mouth trembled and she seemed to deflate in front of Alison's eyes. "But . . . I *am* the queen! Merrie Olde England is built around me!"

Elissa corrected her. "You play a part, like the other people here. You seem to have forgotten that, and you've been treating people worse and worse over the years. I hated to discipline you, because you're an old hand. So I shut my eyes . . . for too long."

"Please . . ." Gwen had wilted; tears filled her eyes. Alison was astonished to find herself feeling sorry for the woman. Some of those watching turned away in embarrassment.

"Elissa . . . I care so much about Merrie Olde England." Gwen grabbed Elissa's hands. "It's so important to me. Don't take it away, please! I'll change! I'll be good, I promise!"

"Let's talk in my office," Elissa said gently.

Gwen nodded, her makeup now streaked with tears, and allowed Elissa to lead her out of the tent.

As they left there was a babble of excited voices. Bonnie leaned toward Alison. "The wicked witch is dead! Way to go, Alison!"

Alison felt too numb to reply.

"Alison, we have to talk," Robin said. "Can we get out of here for a minute?"

"Sure." They left the tent and walked a little way into the trees.

Robin turned to her. "I have to tell you . . . last night I figured there was no point saying this because you don't feel about me the way I feel about you—"

Alison's head began to whirl. "How do you think I feel about you? And how do you feel about me?"

"How do I feel? I love you, Alison! I never said that before, so it's hard for me . . . and then, after you said you weren't interested, I just—"

"Robin, no!" Alison didn't know whether to laugh or cry. She took his hand. "I thought you just wanted to be friends. I was afraid I'd lose you completely, so I didn't tell you I love you, but I do! I love you, Robin!"

Alison saw her love reflected in his eyes. She floated on a cloud of bliss into his arms. They kissed, and time stood still.

"You're so beautiful," he murmured into her hair. "And you're tough . . . standing up to Gwen like that. But how can you love a geek like me?"

She leaned back to contemplate his face and stroke his cheek. "Let's see. I love being with you, you're funny, you make me feel good, Dana thinks you're cute . . . I could give you more reasons— uh-oh, my folks! I promised to meet them, and I'm late!"

Hand in hand they ran to the tent so she could change. Kayla, on her way out, saw them holding hands and her face lit up in a big grin.

"Be right out," said Alison. She beckoned to Kayla and whispered, "You were right and I was wrong."

"I knew it!" Kayla said. "Tell me all about it."

"Later. I have to change and meet my family."

Mr. and Mrs. Crisp were looking around anxiously when Alison ran up with Robin in tow. "Hi," Alison gasped. "Sorry I'm late. Something came up."

"Honey, we had a great time," said her father, "but we have to get going. Are you coming with us?"

"I'll go home with Kayla and her parents." She glanced at Robin. "I'd like to stay around a little longer."

"We'll see you later, then," said Mrs. Crisp. "Robin, I hope we'll be seeing more of you."

Robin smiled. "I hope so, too, Mrs. Crisp."

"Ally?" Dana actually looked cheerful. "Can I come out here with you again?"

"Anytime," Alison answered.

Her father gave her a kiss. "Honey, you looked like a fairy-tale princess today."

"And it's on videotape," added Mrs. Crisp.

Alison and Robin waved to the Crisps as they walked toward the parking lot. "You made Dana laugh," she said. "You *are* a magician."

He put an arm around her waist and grinned at her. "If she thinks I'm cute, it's the least I could do. What do you feel like doing?"

Alison shrugged. It didn't matter to her, as long as they were together. "If Sherwood Forest was open, we could have our archery contest."

"Yeah, too bad. I was going to beat you, too."

"In your dreams!" She jabbed him with an elbow.

"Have you walked the old fire trail?" He pointed to the far end of the path. "It goes through a wildlife preserve."

"Sounds great," Alison said. "Let's go!"

The trail was hemmed in by a forest and

covered with pine needles. Sunlight filtered through the trees, making a pattern of light and shadow all around them. They walked slowly, hand in hand.

"This is great," said Alison, looking around her. "It's like we're a million miles away from—"

She stopped. "What was that noise?"

Robin cocked his head. "I didn't hear anything."

"It sounded like a voice, up ahead."

"Are you sure?" They stood still, listening intently.

Alison shook her head. "I guess I was imagining—"

"Wait! Now I hear it, too! But what is it?"

The noise sounded like someone calling out, but it was oddly indistinct. "Whatever it is," said Alison, "it's off the trail to the left. Maybe it's an animal."

"Let's take a look." They went cautiously forward, looking into the trees as they walked.

The noise came again, just alongside them this time.

Leaving the trail, Alison and Robin climbed over logs, stooped under low-hanging branches, and entered a clearing.

Two men lay tied hand and foot with heavy rope, tape over their mouths. Alison was astonished to recognize Sinclair and Tresh. Tresh's garish shirt had been replaced by a denim workshirt. The men squirmed and tried to speak but the tape muffled their voices.

Suddenly, a steely hand clamped around Alison's arm and spun her around. She stared into the cold eyes of Billy Hawley. "Well, what do you know?" he growled. "You saved me the trouble of coming after you."

He swung her around by the arm, slamming her into a tree. Alison sank to the ground, dazed.

"Leave her alone, Hawley!" shouted Robin.

Gasping, helpless, Alison saw Billy advance on Robin. "I've been looking forward to this," Billy said menacingly. "No one's here to rescue you. It's just you and me."

His right fist connected with Robin's mouth, drawing blood. Robin tried to shake it off, circling away to his right.

Alison fought to clear her head as Billy hit Robin in the midsection. Robin dodged a looping right hand and landed a punch on Billy's nose. Billy plowed forward, trying to wrap his arms around Robin, but the juggler jumped nimbly back.

Billy darted to the edge of the clearing, picked up a club like a policeman's nightstick, and swung at Robin's head. Robin ducked and tried to step back, but he tripped and sprawled on the ground.

Grinning, Billy raised the club. "Juggle this, punk."

"*No!*" Alison screamed, jumping to her feet. She threw herself desperately on Billy's back, grabbing at the stick as he tried to buck her off. Robin leaped up and drove a fist into Billy's stomach. The big man grunted and doubled over.

Robin slammed a knee into Billy's jaw and Billy fell motionless.

"You okay?" Robin asked Alison, breathing hard.

"I'm fine, but what about you? You're bleeding!"

"It's nothing," he snapped. "Let's get Billy tied up while he's out, and see to the other guys."

"What's going on here?" Derek Kimball walked into the clearing, looking around in surprise. He wore jeans and a sweater, and carried a canvas gym bag. It was the first time Alison had seen him out of costume.

"We found these guys tied up," Alison said. "Then, Billy jumped us."

Derek put down his bag. "Jumped you? Billy?" He took the club from Billy's hand. "Did he use this?"

"He tried to," said Robin. "He could've killed me and it wouldn't have bothered him at all."

"I'm shocked!" said Derek, hefting the heavy stick. Abruptly, he pivoted and slammed Robin in the head. Robin dropped to the ground and didn't move.

"Robin!" screamed Alison, throwing herself down at his side. She stared up at Derek. "Are you crazy?"

Derek sighed. "You've been very troublesome." He pulled a revolver out of his bag. "Don't do anything foolish. I'll use this if I have to."

He reached into the bag and removed a coil of heavy rope. "Tie up your boyfriend."

Suddenly Alison understood. "The one behind the sabotage . . . it wasn't Sinclair, it was you!"

"To be fair," answered Derek, "Billy helped, too. He made that horse rear—he jabbed it with a tack while the crowd was watching the procession. I couldn't have cut Alfredo's rope, but it was easy for Billy to do it just before his men strung it across the stage. And while I suggested shooting a customer with a Sherwood Forest arrow, Billy was the archer. He did the shooting last night, too. Wasn't it clever of him to wear that hideous shirt of Mr. Tresh's, in case he was seen?

"I didn't want anyone to actually *die*—what I added to the lemonade and the fruit ices was only to make people sick. But Billy persuaded me that we could arrange for all the blame to fall on Sinclair and Tresh—if they weren't alive to clear matters up. And Billy knew that you were a danger to us because you overheard us making our plans, a few days before the fair opened."

So it wasn't a dream at all, Alison thought. "But why?" she asked, hoping to buy time by making Derek talk. "You love Merrie Olde England. Why destroy it?"

Derek scowled. "I love what it *was:* unspoiled, delightful, simple. Now it's a mockery—soft ice cream, country-western music, all sorts of horrible things. It has to stop."

Keeping the gun on Alison, Derek walked to a clump of bushes and pulled out a gasoline can.

"Merrie Olde England will burn to the ground so a pure Merrie Olde England can rise from the ashes.

Alas, the bodies of the villains who set the fire—a greedy developer and his henchman—will be found in the rubble, caught in their own deadly scheme."

Sinclair and Tresh began thrashing frantically, straining, wild-eyed, against their bonds.

Billy groaned and began to stir.

"Good, he's coming around," Derek said. "Alison, I told you to tie Robin up."

"You're going to kill us, too?" Alison felt a surge of fear. Derek wasn't just a harmless eccentric. He was crazy and dangerous.

"We must. You're a danger to us," Derek replied. "And Billy insists—he doesn't like you at all."

"I know why you did this," said Alison, desperately trying to prolong the conversation and fighting off an urge to panic. "But what's Billy's interest?"

Derek grinned. "Billy doesn't care about the finer things, so I gave him a lot of money. I'm quite well off, you know. Now stop stalling and tie him up."

Alison stood by Robin, rope in hand, then threw it down. "I won't help you. Do it yourself."

"I will," snapped Derek. "After I shoot you."

He walked toward Alison, glowering. "You're determined to be a nuisance right to the end."

Suddenly, Robin lunged forward, driving a shoulder into Derek's knees and making him stagger. Alison snatched Derek's gun arm and sank her teeth into his wrist. Derek screamed and dropped the gun, and Robin grabbed it.

A few minutes later, Derek and Billy sat against a tree while Robin covered them with the gun. Alison pulled the tape from the mouths of Sinclair and Tresh.

"You saved our lives." Sinclair's voice shook.

"What happened?" asked Alison.

Sinclair glared at Billy. "Yesterday, he offered to help me get the land. He asked us to meet him here, where we could talk in private. Then he clobbered us with that club, and trussed us up like turkeys."

"We were here all night!" Tresh glared at Sinclair. "Thanks for getting me mixed up in this!"

"We don't have a knife," said Robin. "We'll get the police to cut you free and take these two away. They're all over the fair today, looking for you."

"For me? How did they know we were being held captive?" Sinclair asked.

"They didn't," Alison replied. "They think you two are responsible for the dirty tricks around here."

Tresh groaned. "Great! I'm a wanted man, I ache all over, and my favorite shirt is gone. I should've stayed in Akron."

"After all, Mr. Sinclair," Robin pointed out, "you *were* heard threatening Elissa."

"I was trying to scare her into being reasonable," protested Sinclair. "It was good business strategy."

"Yeah, right," grumbled Tresh.

"Who are you?" Alison asked Tresh.

"The genius's brother-in-law. I'm a druggist,

here on vacation. Eric said, 'Come to the fair with me while I do some business. It'll be fun.' Fun!"

Sinclair sighed. "Mitch, what can I say?"

"Nothing! These things don't happen in Akron."

"I'm sorry, all right?"

Tresh snorted. "Sorry! I loved that shirt."

"Why don't I get the police?" suggested Alison.

"Good idea," Robin answered. "And hurry, or I may have to gag these two again."

It was after six, MOE had closed for the day, and the police had arrested Derek and Billy. Alison and Robin sat together on a hay bale by the main stage, with Elissa, Zach, and the Martínez family.

"Business will be much better next week," said Mr. Martínez, putting an arm around his wife.

"I'll see that the media knows our troubles are over," Elissa assured them.

"What about Gwen? Was she fired?" asked Alison.

Elissa smiled. "She asked for another chance. She said she'd make apologies and clean up her act. I think she'll do it."

"Well, it's time to hit the road," said Mrs. Martínez.

Robin took Alison's hand. "I'll walk you out."

"Kayla, can you give us a hand with our gear?" said Mr. Martínez. "Alison, we'll meet you at the van."

Alison and Robin said good-bye to Elissa and Zach and walked hand in hand toward the parking lot.

"So," said Robin, "do you want to have that archery contest next Saturday? Sherwood Forest will be open."

"You're on," Alison said, twining her fingers in his. "What do I get if I win?"

Robin faced her and gently put a hand under her chin. "You get a kiss. And if *I* win—"

"Then you get one," she whispered, brushing his lips with hers. "And if it's a tie . . ."

"Then we divide the prize," he said. "How does that sound to you?"

Alison clasped him around the neck with both hands. "It sounds perfect."

You won't want to miss . . .

YOU CAN NEVER GO HOME AGAIN
DYAN SHELDON

It's a romance made in purgatory.

When Angel's parents split up, she's forced to move to a ramshackle cottage that's a total comedown from the upscale home she grew up in. Far from her popular crowd—and her boyfriend—Angel thinks life couldn't get much worse. Then she meets B.J., a smartmouthed biker with big, soulful eyes. The only reason B.J.'s not the greaser from hell is that he hasn't been able to get that far. Instead, he's been perfecting his bad attitude since 1959—when he died and his ghost took up residence in the attic of Angel's new house.

She can't kiss him because she hates his guts, and she can't kill him because he's already dead. Angel thinks she needs B.J. like she needs a hole in the head, but she's wrong. B.J. might be able to help Angel—if only she'll let him.

0-8167-3691-X • $3.50 U.S.

Available wherever you buy books.

And it's sequel . . .

SAVE THE LAST DANCE FOR ME
DYAN SHELDON

How can someone who's dead seem so alive?

So what if B.J. saved Angel's life once before? He's still got a major attitude problem, and Angel wishes he'd act more like what he is, a dead guy, than the pain-in-the-neck big brother he seems to think he is. Worse than his constant snooping and dumb advice and rude remarks about the guys she's interested in, now B.J.'s beginning to act dopey about Angel's best friend, Suze.

What is it with him and Suze anyway? Angel knows B.J.'s nothing more than a cheap hood who died during a robbery attempt. But Suze thinks he's been misunderstood, a rebel and a loner who took the rap to protect someone else. Angel's happy enough to leave a decades-old mystery alone, but Suze has come up with the perfect incentive: if the girls find out the truth, maybe B.J.'s ghost can find peace at last—and stop bugging Angel.

0-8167-3794-0 • $3.95 U.S.

Available wherever you buy books.

A.G. Cascone

IN A CROOKED LITTLE HOUSE

. . . lived a twisted little man

People are dying at Huntington Prep. A fall down the stairs, a drowning, a fatal bump on the head. It could happen anywhere. But Iggy-Boy knows these aren't accidents. Now he's set his sights on beautiful Casey, the nicest girl in school. She's in terrible danger, but she doesn't know it. She doesn't even know Iggy-Boy exists. But Iggy-Boy is someone she knows, someone nearby, someone who's watching her every move . . .

0-8167-3532-8 • $3.50 U.S.

Available wherever you buy books.